A FISHERMAN'S DREAM

Arthinkal

To all the dreamers throughout the land.

CONTENTS

JOIN MY MAILING LIST

Hey there!

Join my mailing list to receive a free copy of the first book in the *Life in Kornur Series*, *Untouchable Lives: A Novella*, by visiting https://arthinkal.substack.com/p/free-ebook-untouchable-lives-a-novella

You can also join my mailing list by subscribing to my weekly newsletter for new book updates and to receive my essays and articles in your inbox: https://arthinkal.substack.com/ (You can unsubscribe at any time if you wish to do so).

The newsletter publishes essays and articles on literature, music, art, history, philosophy, politics, law, and social issues, all written by me. If you would like to receive my essays and articles and support my work, please feel free to subscribe.

As an independent writer, your subscription and support would be greatly appreciated.

Thank you!

Regards,

Arthinkal

CHAPTER 1

The rickshaw reached and halted at the abandoned garden's gate. Aryan got down. It was six-thirty now and he had another half an hour to go before his duty would begin. He paid the driver and then the rickshaw started away.

He walked toward the rusty gate and saw it was locked from the other side. He looked at the small cabin on the left and he could see the dim orange light inside through the window but he could not see the watchman sitting in there.

The watchman must be there inside, he thought. The gate blocked his view and he tried to look through the window again but still he could not see anyone. It was almost dark now and the sky was in transition. The sun had already set and its dying light that remained was slowly disappearing as the air got cooler.

Aryan stood there in front of the gate and banged at it to get the watchman's attention. It did not work. A swarm of mosquitoes hovered right above his head and he tried to dismiss them with his hand. The mosquitoes scattered away for a few seconds and then returned without him even realizing it. Finally he shouted, "Is anyone there? Watchman!"

Suddenly there was some movement inside the cabin and he noticed it. Looking at the window he saw the watchman's head slowly creep out of the window. The orange light inside had been totally eclipsed by the man's head. He heard the man opening the cabin door and he kept his smile ready to greet the grumpy man. The man walked over to the gate and looked at Aryan through it and instantly recognized him.

"Oh! You have come already!" the watchman said, sounding happy.

Aryan was perplexed by the man's sudden kindness. He was not expecting this much warmth from the man.

"Wait a minute, let me open the gate," said the watchman, and then he walked over to a smaller side gate which was beside the main gate and opened it.

"Come, come," the watchman said with a smile.

"Thank you," Aryan said, still confused. What had happened to him? Aryan wondered. Why was he behaving so nice today?

Aryan walked in and looked around and what he saw was a little scary to him. The garden looked dark and foreboding and it had an eerie look about it. It looked like a haunted place. There were no lights inside. The only light that existed there was the orange light inside the cabin. All around was darkness. The thick messy vegetation that had grown inside could not be seen anymore even from where he was standing. No trees and no plants and no benches, nothing. Everything was lost somewhere deep in the darkness and nothing could be seen at all.

He did not walk further ahead. He was a little afraid to take another step as he stared into the darkness ahead. Noises could be heard coming from somewhere inside the darkness. Maybe from the trees or the plants, he thought. He heard the crying of bats and saw a couple of them flying above swiftly but discreetly. He could hear the cries of insects too but he did not know which ones and he did not care to guess.

The watchman sensed his fear and said, "Don't worry, it just looks scary here. But it's really not."

Aryan nodded mechanically. "Okay," he said.

"Follow me," the watchman said and walked ahead of him. Aryan quickly followed him.

The watchman walked in the dark without any difficulty at all. Aryan looked down and around, struggling to find the ground beneath his feet. He walked carefully, almost afraid to increase his pace, and he tried to adjust his eyes to the darkness.

"The boss had come here the day before," said the watchman while walking. "He told me you would be here today for the night shift and that I must show you around."

Aryan walked slowly, searching the ground.

"I was very happy to hear that," the watchman continued. "I thought you were after my shift. But now I know you were not."

The watchman looked behind at Aryan and laughed. He continued to walk with ease. Aryan laughed a faint laugh in return. So that was it, Aryan said to himself. That was why he was so nice to him today. He was no longer threatened.

Aryan smiled.

"I never thought of taking your job," Aryan said.

"I know, I know," the watchman said. "I felt bad for suspecting you. In this city you never know what's going to happen. This is my only job, my only income. And I have a family to look after. You understand right?"

"Yes," Aryan said. "I understand."

He did understand. He understood it very well for he had been in that situation before and it was not a pleasant situation to be in.

"And I don't think anyone will give me another job," the watchman continued. "I have no education or anything. And over here no one cares about you or your family or your troubles and difficulties. No one. Not even the bosses. You have to look out for yourself and help yourself. Everything is about money here. This city didn't become the financial capital of the country for no reason. It runs for money and it runs on money. Money is its blood, its fuel. That's why it exists. Take that as a lesson."

"I will," Aryan said.

He was very smart, Aryan thought. He was not as naive and simple as he looked. He knew this city well. He knew how this city worked and how it survived and thrived. This city was ruthless and this watchman knew it. That was why he was so protective of his job and had felt so threatened.

They reached a small concrete shed which was at the far end of the garden. The watchman searched for the key and then opened the door of the shed in the darkness. He took one step in and switched on the light inside and a bright yellow bulb immediately lit up and the room inside came into existence. Aryan walked in after the watchman.

"Here it is," the watchman said.

Aryan looked around the small room which was even smaller and more cramped up than his house in Kornur. But he did not mind it. It was fairly clean and organized so that it gave him the impression that it was all done up very recently. Along the walls were kept old gardening tools which might have been used extensively in the past. They were lying there like relics of the past, rusted and worn out and broken or dismantled.

Aryan walked along the walls of the small room inspecting the tools carefully with a keen eye. He noticed that almost all the tools were rusted. No wonder the room had a faint smell of rust, he thought. But it was manageable.

The room was bright-yellow in color because

of the light from the yellow bulb. Aryan walked over to the center of the room away from the walls and here it was nice and clean and there was enough space for him to sleep or sit. And that was all he wanted for now. At least there would be a proper roof over his head, he thought. And the shed was of concrete, strong enough to bear all kinds of weather.

He thought of his small brick house in Kornur which was near the sea and not far from the market. It had never been painted from the inside or the outside just like all the other houses in Kornur. The front door of the house opened up to a narrow dirt street right outside and the back door opened up to a narrower gully that usually flowed with dirty soapy water as the residents washed their clothes there. The house had no rooms but it had two small windows, one near the kitchen and the other near the bed, and it had one cramped-up toilet to the side.

He remembered the old rusty bed, the rusty cupboard, the old chair, the noisy fan, the dim yellow bulb for light, and the rudimentary kitchen on the floor that could barely be called a kitchen with its stove and few cooking vessels and ladles and three steel plates and a steel glass for water and a small low wooden stool which was used to sit on while cooking. He remembered it all and smiled.

"And there's your mattress and pillow and there's the stove," the watchman said, pointing in their direction at the wall behind the opened door.

Aryan turned around and looked in the direction in which the man was pointing. He saw an old thin mattress on the floor and a pillow on top of it, and on top of that two sets of his uniform. And beside that was kept the stove.

"There are a few utensils in that small shelf there," said the watchman, pointing at the shelf.

Aryan walked over to the shelf and opened it. There were two steel plates, one steel glass, a wooden ladle, a tube of mosquito repellent cream, and five small matchboxes. Aryan nodded after inspecting them.

"And the boss says if you need anything at all you must let him know," the watchman said.

Aryan nodded.

"He's a good man, our boss," the watchman said.

"I know," Aryan said and smiled. Then he asked, "Why don't they start the garden again?"

"That question can't be answered by simple men like us," said the watchman. "There are a lot of problems. It's very complicated."

Aryan nodded. "Is it illegal?" he asked.

"I don't know. But it's disputed. I try not to ask the boss too many questions here. I just do my job and mind my own business. I salute the boss whenever he shows up and I salute him when he leaves."

The watchman smiled at Aryan as if he had indirectly revealed to him the secret to a happy life. Mind your own business and do not ask unnecessary questions. Those were the golden rules.

Aryan smiled back at him and nodded. This watchman was really smart and shrewd, he thought.

"I suggest you do the same," the watchman said and walked out of the door. Then he stood there and looked at Aryan.

"I will," Aryan said.

The watchman started to walk away and Aryan began closing the door. Then he remembered something.

"Wait a minute!" Aryan called out to the watchman.

The watchman turned around and looked at Aryan.

"I don't know your name," Aryan said.

The watchman smiled and said, "Ganesh. And yours?"

"Aryan."

"Aryan," Ganesh said and smiled, and then he turned around and walked away.

CHAPTER 2

Five years had passed since Aryan had started living the life of a fisherman.

He was twenty-one now and did not study anymore. He had stopped his studies five years ago. It had not been his choice to quit his education but circumstances had led him to do it. And for the past five years he had led the same life that his father had once led, which was a life he had always dreaded.

He got up at five in the morning every single day and got ready immediately. He then consumed a light breakfast and drank a cup of strong tea. And then he left for the day.

He walked from his house to the shore in the cool morning darkness carrying all his fishing equipment with him. On the way there he met the other fishermen who accompanied him into the open sea and then they all got into their small boats and started out together.

They rowed and rowed farther away from the shore and then they spread out widely and reserved large spaces for them to fish in. They spent hours on end in the open waters under the torturing sun trying to catch as many fish as possible and then they returned to the shore by mid-morning. They sorted out their catch near the shore itself and then they headed straight for the market, and in the market they would stay for the rest of the day until ten or ten-thirty at night selling their catch.

He had no time for drawing or painting anymore and he had no time to dream of becoming an artist. But occasionally, while he sat in his small boat in the middle of the open sea patiently waiting for a big catch his thoughts slowly but inevitably drifted toward painting. He imagined how different his life would have been if he had become an artist. Sometimes he thought of picking up a paintbrush again someday. He would then impulsively make a promise to himself that one day he would start painting again. But he had no idea when that day would actually arrive.

Deep down inside he had always known that becoming an artist was exactly what he wanted to do in life. He never had any ambition of becoming a fisherman like his father and he had no desire to live a mundane and colorless life like his parents had. He could never bear the thought of waking up early every morning to take a small boat into the sea in order to catch fish and then come back to shore and sell those fish until the end of the day. He had always abhorred that lifestyle for it seemed to be a terribly boring life to him.

And so he had always wanted to fulfill his

dream of becoming an artist even though he knew that it was a foolish idea. No one in his entire village had ever done such a thing before as painting was considered a rare hobby there and not a viable trade or profession. He had also known quite well that not a single soul would have agreed with him that it was a good and plausible idea. Everyone would have ridiculed it, he was sure of that.

So he had decided to keep it a secret. But when he turned sixteen he found out that fate had other things in store for him, diverting the course of his life in a whole new direction.

But there was no sense in thinking about all those things now. Those things belonged to the distant past and he only allowed himself to think of his past when he sat alone in his boat, just him and his solitude. It was already too late. He was a fisherman now and a fisherman he would remain.

CHAPTER 3

It was six-fifty now. In ten minutes Aryan's duty would begin. He looked at the folded mattress above which the pillow and the two sets of uniforms were kept. He picked up one set and quickly changed into it.

The uniform was black in color and it looked as if it had been used before. He immediately spotted a few food stains on it but he paid no attention to them. For him the uniform was new. He was quite happy with it. It was not much faded and so it looked as good as new from afar.

Aryan walked out of the shed and closed the door behind him and then he began walking toward the little cabin where Ganesh was sitting. He walked in the dark, still afraid, but he forced himself to continue. He could see better in the dark now, not finding it as difficult as the first time.

He had to be brave for this job, he said to himself. That was the skill required. And he had to become brave soon, he thought, for otherwise he would not be able to survive in this job. If he could not even walk from his shed to the cabin in the dark how could he expect himself to defend the garden from those delinquents? he asked himself. He could not, he answered. He had to stop being so scared and be a man, he told himself as he walked toward the cabin.

He managed to walk perfectly well, even dodging a big stone at the right time. His eyes were properly adjusted now and he walked with much ease just like how Ganesh had. He reached the cabin and knocked on the door thrice. Ganesh immediately opened the door.

"Come in," Ganesh said.

Aryan nodded and entered the cabin. His head was almost touching the ceiling and he refrained from looking up for fear of hitting his head. As he had expected, the cabin was small and congested and was lit by a small orange bulb. It had space for two people to sit but there was only one plastic chair inside on which Ganesh was sitting comfortably. An old worn-down wooden shelf sat in one corner. An old clock hung on the wall. There was a steel stool which was almost completely rusted and it was used as a table. A big dirty plastic bottle with water in it was kept on the stool.

"You can also keep your feet on it," Ganesh said and then started demonstrating it to Aryan.

He picked up the dirty bottle from the stool and placed it down on the floor and then he lifted both his feet up and placed them on the stool and then started shaking them casually. Then he looked up at Aryan and smiled proudly. Aryan looked back at him and then at his shaking feet.

Then he laughed.

"You can do it too," said Ganesh happily. "Don't worry. I will teach you everything. But it's time for me to leave now. It's your turn. It's seven already."

Aryan smiled and nodded. Ganesh stood up.

"Oh wait, I forgot to give you the two most important things required for this job," Ganesh said. "One minute."

He opened the small wooden shelf and fidgeted inside, searching for something. Then he found what he was looking for.

He brought out a big silver torch and handed it over to Aryan without looking at him. Aryan took the torch from his hand and began inspecting it. Ganesh went back to fidgeting inside the shelf again, searching for something else now.

Aryan looked at the torch carefully. He was very impressed for the torch looked new. This was the first item here that seemed to be new, he thought. Then he switched it on but nothing happened. No light came from it. He tried again, and again nothing happened.

"Ah! Here it is," Ganesh said aloud and brought out a box full of batteries. "Here are the batteries for the torch. All unused batteries are in this box, so keep it back safely inside this shelf. Whenever the torch battery gets over throw the old ones and take new ones from this box. And always keep the box back in."

"Alright," said Aryan.

"We have a very important job, you know,"

Ganesh said seriously. "And for us to be able to discharge our duty properly we must have a torch that's always functioning. That's why we keep a stock of batteries, so we never run out of batteries."

"I see," Aryan said softly, slightly confused by Ganesh's seriousness.

"Now you can put the batteries in your torch. Try and see if it works properly."

Aryan did as he was told. He put the batteries in the torch and switched it on and a strong bright round beam of yellow light came out from it and hit Ganesh straight in the eye. Ganesh immediately flinched in panic and turning his eyes away from the powerful beam of light he said loudly, "Be careful! Be careful! It hurts the eye. It can be dangerous."

Aryan panicked and turned the torch away and then switched it off.

"I'm sorry," Aryan said. "I didn't know it was that powerful."

Ganesh carefully looked up again. Then he said, "That's fine. It happens. Now you know why it's so important."

Aryan nodded.

"An intruder would run away rather than face this torch," said Ganesh. "And now the other important thing."

"Yes."

"The stick," Ganesh said and brought out a thick wooden stick from behind the door. He handed it over to Aryan horizontally, with both hands, as if he were handing over an emperor's sword.

"This is yours to use," Ganesh said with a big smile.

Aryan received it in the same way he was offered it, horizontally and with both hands. The stick felt heavy in his hand, it felt strong. It would definitely hurt anyone who was hit with it. Aryan's confidence grew all of a sudden.

"That's no ordinary stick, my friend," Ganesh said proudly. "If you hit someone with it, it can break his bones. I have done it in the past."

"To whom?" Aryan asked.

"It doesn't matter," Ganesh said quickly. "That's not at all important. What's important is that you must use it wisely. But when it is absolutely necessary, take God's name and use it freely without any worries."

"Okay."

"But never on the head. It is strong enough to break the skull and kill the man."

"Never on the head," Aryan repeated.

"Yes. On the legs is fine. On the back too. Hands, sometimes. But try to avoid it on the hands if possible."

"Got it," Aryan said.

"Are you strong enough to swing it properly?"

"I think so."

"Good. Keep these two things with you at all times. Understand?"

"Understood."

Ganesh smiled at Aryan. Aryan looked at him in anticipation, waiting for him to continue talking. But Ganesh did not say anything further. He put his hand into his right trouser pocket and took out a big bunch of old keys.

"Look here," Ganesh said. "There are ten keys in this bunch. But don't worry, you need to use only two. One key for the side gate from which you enter and leave and the other one for the cabin door. The other eight keys are of no use to you."

"Okay," Aryan said, nodding.

"And always leave the main gate locked. Never open it. You must only use the side gate."

Aryan nodded again. "Any tips?" he asked.

"Oh, it's easy," Ganesh said, and then he picked up a plastic bag in which he had a few things of his and walked out of the cabin. Aryan followed him out. They reached the gate and stopped. The gate was already open.

"Use the torch and the stick to intimidate them if they don't listen. It will work. Hit the ground with the stick a few times when you warn them. It will scare them away. And don't worry about the rest. Just remember God and you will be fine."

Aryan nodded but he did not say anything.

"Now listen," said Ganesh. "It's a serious job but you will get used to it. Always remember we are doing this for a good cause. We are protecting our society by doing this."

Aryan could see by the look on Ganesh's

face that he was serious. He honestly believed that they were doing a great service to society. Maybe they really were, Aryan thought. Maybe he had underestimated the importance of watchmen. When he thought about it he found that Ganesh was absolutely right. They were protecting their society in whatever small way possible. It was true.

Why were they not given enough credit for their service? Aryan wondered. It was unfair. There was much more to being a watchman than he had imagined. It was a noble profession when done properly and sincerely, he said to himself. They deserved respect and more credit for their work.

He was so wrong about it, he thought. He had belittled the profession and he should not have done that. And now he suddenly felt a surge of pride within him. He felt proud to be a watchman. Did his theory make any sense? he asked himself. He was not so sure but he hoped it did.

"Sure it may get boring at times," Ganesh continued, "just sitting there doing nothing in particular. But remember your duty, your responsibility. Stay alert. Be brave."

Aryan nodded mechanically. Ganesh spoke like a military general going to war, he thought. Everything for him was about duty and responsibility and a sense of purpose and about the greater good. He made it sound like some mission or some great battle, Aryan thought and smiled. Did he really believe all that he said? Aryan wondered. Or was he just saying it for the heck of it? Or maybe the boss had told him to say all this.

"And anyway, the most serious danger to you will come from mosquitoes, not humans," Ganesh said. "There are many here. Look above your head."

Aryan looked above his head and saw a swarm of busy mosquitoes. Then he looked above Ganesh's head and saw the same. He swiped his hand over his head and the mosquitoes dispersed temporarily.

"No use in doing that," Ganesh said. "They will return. They always return. So be careful. Always apply the mosquito repellent cream before coming out for your duty. That's as important as the torch and the stick. Remember that."

"I will," said Aryan. "What's the boss' name?"

"I don't know," Ganesh said and smiled. "I just call him Boss."

Aryan smiled back. "Alright," he said.

"I shall see you tomorrow morning," Ganesh said, and then he turned and walked away.

Aryan went into the little cabin and sat down on the plastic chair. He picked up the dirty bottle from the floor and inspected it to make sure the water inside was clean. He was satisfied. Only the bottle looked dirty, he decided. Then he proceeded to swallow down the water without touching his mouth to the mouth of the bottle. Then he placed the bottle on the stool and sat back on his chair and stared outside the window.

CHAPTER 4

One night Aryan got back home from the market and found all his old paintings neatly placed in one corner of the house. These were paintings made by him in his teenage years, already reflecting the skill of an experienced painter and the promise of a great future ahead. He had forgotten about them.

When he had finally decided to become a fisherman he had put them all away into the attic for he did not need a daily reminder of what he had to give up and what he had lost.

He was perplexed by their sudden appearance. He started examining them. Then he looked around for his mother but did not find her. He continued examining them, slowly falling into the deadly trap of nostalgia.

His mother came up from the backside of the house where she had been washing clothes and saw him looking at the paintings.

"Oh, you are back. I didn't even realize," she said casually.

He turned and looked at her.

"Ma, why did you remove these paintings from the attic?" he said.

"Oh yes, I forgot to tell you," she said. "I was clearing the attic in the afternoon and I came across these paintings. I thought you must have forgotten about them."

Aryan did not respond. He was looking at the paintings. He felt a slight pain, a burning sensation in his heart. The pain of nostalgia it was. He remembered his early teenage years when everything was fine and everything was normal and when he still had a dream he truly believed in. But everything had changed. Everything was different now.

"Anyway, I wanted to suggest something to you," she said. "Why don't you try and sell these paintings? I'm sure there will be someone who would be interested in buying them. And God knows we could use some of that extra money you may end up earning."

He looked at her, surprised by her suggestion. He tried to figure out if she was serious. She was, he decided.

"I don't think so, Ma," he said. "No one would pay to buy these old paintings."

"Don't say that," she retorted immediately. "I'm sure someone would be interested in buying them. And there's no harm in at least trying to sell them, is there?"

Aryan turned his head and stared at the paintings. He was considering it. He remained silent.

Then he said softly, "No, I guess not."

She smiled.

"Good," she said. "Anyway, there's no place in the attic now. I stuffed a few things in there."

"I thought so," he said and shook his head.

"Yes. So you might as well try and sell them," she said.

Aryan sat there still wondering if anyone would really buy his paintings. And after giving it some serious thought he finally decided to give it a go. After all he had nothing to lose. Nothing at all.

He decided that he would display his paintings on a small table right next to where he sat in his usual place in the market to sell fish.

CHAPTER 5

Five hours passed by slowly and painfully. Aryan still sat there in the little cabin with his feet on the rusted stool and half-asleep. He had been in this state of half-asleep and half-awake for more than an hour. His usual sleeping time had passed by and he had entered a wholly different territory now, an uncharted one.

It was five minutes past midnight. Aryan had very rarely stayed awake till this late at night. He felt uncomfortable. His head was heavy with sleep and his eyes were shutting involuntarily. He forced himself many times to keep his eyes open but he barely succeeded at it. He splashed a little water on his face from the dirty water bottle whenever he felt like he was about to fall asleep. But the effect did not last long enough for within five minutes he would be on the verge of falling asleep again. He tried slapping himself a couple of times too but that did not work either. It only caused him pain.

He was bored too, bored like never before, bored to such an extent that he was prepared to quit not because of the sleep but because of the boredom. There was absolutely nothing to do there and all he could do was sit and stare into the surrounding darkness and at the gate and at anything that moved and at things that did not exist and at nothing at all.

Other than the occasional shrieks of bats and the cries of owls and insects he heard nothing. Nothing at all. The silence bothered him for not a soul stirred in that place during that time. The air was perfectly still and cool and it did not move or blow. No wind existed there. After four hours in the midst of this silence he could not even hear himself breathe. He felt as if he had lost his sense of hearing. He thought he had turned deaf.

Every hour he got up and walked outside the cabin with his torch and stick in either hand. He walked up and down near the gate to warm his legs up and to normalize the blood flow in them. He also did it to avoid being bit by the wild mosquitoes. Those short walks in the dark gave him great relief.

This struggle of his had started around eleven, the time he usually went to bed. And it was continuing now, only getting much worse. This job was much more challenging than he had anticipated. He felt quite foolish for underestimating it. It was not at all easy for him.

But the thing that bothered him the most, almost to an unbearable extent, was the danger that Ganesh had warned him about, the danger from mosquitoes. He had forgotten to apply the cream and had only realized it an hour after being continuously bit by them. Then he walked back to his shed and took out the cream from the shelf and applied it generously over his hands and face. Then he went back to the cabin.

These mosquitoes were relentless, he said to himself. They never gave up and ran away and they never got tired. They persisted and persisted no matter how many of them were killed or how many times they were swiped away or no matter where one was they were always there and they always came back.

In his state of boredom and sleep he began thinking. If one thought about it deep enough one would see that mosquitoes were fearless creatures, not afraid of anything or anyone, he thought. They were all willing to die for their cause, the cause of sucking the blood out of other creatures. And they were relentless in their pursuit of that cause. The whole world was against them, wanting to eliminate them, but still they persisted and survived and thrived.

And why did they suck our blood after all? he asked himself. Were they not doing it for their own survival? Yes they were. That was exactly why they did it. They did it to survive. They attacked us for their own survival just as how we attacked other creatures for our own survival.

So what right did we have to label them as bad? What right did we have to judge them? What difference was there between them and us? Did we not kill animals to eat? And did we not eat to survive? Mosquitoes did the very same thing and they did it with much more risk to their life than when we did it. So clearly we had no moral standing over them, he thought. We were no better than them.

Aryan smiled and stopped thinking. He laughed silently for a few moments. He laughed at himself. What was he even thinking about? he questioned himself. Who thought of such silly stuff? He was going crazy over here, he said to himself and laughed again. He found it funny. He had just philosophized on mosquitoes and he had done it with utter seriousness. It was all crazy talk. It must be the sleep and the silence and darkness that were making him crazy, he decided.

He himself hated mosquitoes. He despised them and wished to eliminate each and every one of them. He wished to drive them into extinction never to return again. He smiled at his own foolishness. He could be so weird at times, he told himself.

He forced himself to stop thinking about mosquitoes and then he forced himself to stop thinking at all. After five minutes he fell asleep.

CHAPTER 6

Aryan returned to shore by mid-morning and went straight to his house instead of going to the market. He took only six of his paintings to display them at the market. If he was successful at selling those six paintings only then would he try to sell the rest of them, he thought.

He arrived at the market half an hour later than usual. Then he set up a small table beside him which was barely big enough to keep three paintings on it even though the paintings were fairly small in size. The other three paintings he kept at the foot of the table, and after much thought he decided to sell each painting for five hundred rupees.

Now all he had to do was wait and watch.

Till mid-afternoon no one had really bothered to ask about his paintings. But that was mainly because not many people showed up at the market in the afternoons. Customers were very rare between two to four in the afternoon as the sun was too strong and uncomfortable then. They preferred staying at home to rest and sleep rather than venture out into the hot and sunny streets.

There was a daily lull in the market around that time.

And so those two hours provided the fish sellers with a much-needed break to have lunch and to relax under some shade. They all ate at almost the same time and then they sat idle at their stalls and talked and gossiped with each other. Some of them preferred to sleep at their stalls on a mat or on a sheet of plastic with a cloth covering their faces to protect them from the intense glare of the afternoon sun.

On this particular day Aryan was too distracted by his thoughts to talk or sleep. He sat at his stall and thought about his paintings. He thought about his life and how it had changed so quickly and abruptly.

Five years ago he had a dream of becoming an artist. And he had hope then. He had hoped to avoid the life that he now lived. How fate had toyed with him, he wondered. How it had played him wrong and messed with him. How it had messed with his whole life.

He thought about the very event that had diverted the course of his life when he was only sixteen. He thought of that dreadful incident that took place five years ago, the death of his father.

He remembered that day very well. He remembered it vividly and clearly and in great detail as if it had happened only recently, as if it were something that belonged to the recent past and not to a distant one. He remembered each and every word exchanged and everything he saw and each and every emotion involved and every feeling that had risen within him and everything he had experienced.

On this rare occasion he permitted himself to think of his past and to recollect that life-changing, heart-breaking, fearful incident. His heart began to beat rapidly. His palms turned sweaty. He began to relive it like it was some dramatic play being acted out in front of his eyes. A play he had seen many times before again and again with the same clarity.

His friend Raja had come to his school and informed him of his father's death. His father had drowned at sea, Raja had told him. He had been instantly struck with terror. He had failed to comprehend what he had been told. He had refused to believe the news.

Then the two of them ran back to his house. A crowd had already gathered in and around the house. He heard some women crying and wailing. He saw curious little children trying to understand the whole situation with their unformed minds. He saw men trying to comfort their wives in silence.

As he walked toward his house the chaotic crowd parted before him. People tried to console him but he did not bother responding. He was not in a state to respond.

He entered his house and saw the scene in front of him. The scene he had been so afraid to see. He saw his father laid out on the floor lifeless. His clothes were still completely wet and sticking to his bloated and lifeless body. The doctor sat beside the dead body on one side and on the other side he saw his mother sitting and weeping, unable to control herself.

She was being consoled by some neighbors. He walked up to her and he stood there and looked down at his father's body. She looked up and saw him standing and looking down in complete shock. The moment their eyes met there was no need to say anything at all. She knew by the look on his face that he was aware of everything. No words were exchanged between them, none at all.

She got up and embraced her son as tightly as she could and he embraced her back. And then they cried on each other's shoulder.

In spite of all the neighbors present there who were willing to lend their unconditional support both mother and son felt completely alone and isolated from the world. They realized at that terrible moment that no matter how many people were present there then, trying their best to console them, they were still all alone. That sudden realization that they had was like an epiphany. They only had each other now, just mother and son.

The death of his father meant that he had to start working soon so that he could earn enough money for his and his mother's survival. His father's death was so sudden that he found himself utterly ignorant and unprepared to face life ahead. And to make matters worse he lacked all skills other than drawing and painting.

At first he thought about starting his career as an artist in order to earn some money. He knew he was good at it but he was not so naive. He was surprisingly practical and realistic about it all. He was aware of the fact that he could not just become a professional artist overnight and start earning money immediately. It was something that would take many years to achieve if at all he would ever achieve that.

But he did not have many years. He did not even have many days. For if he would not start earning soon he and his mother would go hungry. They already lived an almost hand-to-mouth existence with barely enough savings to last for more than a week.

He could not think of anything that he could possibly do to start earning some money immediately. But his mother had thought of something and so had his neighbors. He had no choice but to become a fisherman just like his father and his grandfather before him, they thought, and it seemed inevitable even to him.

He had discussed the matter with his mother the very night his father had died and the end of that conversation had symbolized and solidified the end of his dreams.

CHAPTER 7

The gate clanked and rattled. Aryan woke up from his sleep. He sat up straight and looked around the cabin. He was not sure what he was looking for. He was a little dazed and lost.

He quickly looked at the clock on the wall. It was almost one-thirty. He thought he had heard something but he was not so sure whether he had heard it in his sleep or in reality. There was silence now.

Aryan continued to sit up straight, almost afraid to stand up. He did not look outside the window yet for he was afraid he would see someone. Then he heard whispers, soft but quick ones. There were many of them. He tried to concentrate on the whispers by reducing the sound of his breathing. He listened carefully. The whispers became more chaotic and he could tell they were coming from multiple sources. But he could not exactly hear the words yet. He waited in attention.

The gate clanked again and now Aryan looked outside the window, finally gaining the courage to do so. He saw them. Four of them. No, five of them.

Black figures against the orange street light trying to climb over the gate and into the garden.

Two of them had started climbing the gate. They climbed carefully, the other three helping them up. The two climbing were fat and bulky. They clearly needed the help of the others. The other three black forms were rather thin and agile-looking. They could climb over on their own without any help.

Aryan panicked for a moment. His heart began to pound rapidly. His palms were sweaty again and he quickly wiped them against his pants. He picked up the torch and held it in his left hand and then he picked up the stick and held it in his right hand which was his stronger hand. His heart pounded away. He was nervous now. His hands shivered and he tried to steady them.

He had never had such a confrontation with anyone before. Such physical confrontations were entirely against his nature. It scared him. It made him nervous. And all these feelings suddenly hit him all at once and he was completely unprepared to handle them.

The two bulky figures had almost reached the top of the gate now. Aryan knew he could not waste any more time. If he had to stop them it had to be done now. He could not allow them to cross over to the other side of the gate. He would have failed in his duty then and that was one thing he could not tolerate. He must not fail in his duty, he said to himself. He was protecting his society, he reminded himself again although he was not truly convinced about it.

This pep talk served to increase his confidence a little. His hands steadied and his grip on the stick and the torch tightened. They fit perfectly in his hands now. His palms were slowly turning dry and his heart began to pound less vigorously. But the thrill of action now persisted within him, intensifying as the time for it came nearer.

They had to be stopped immediately, he told himself. He thought quickly for one last time. It was a deliberate call to think. And he thought quickly but clearly. Would the advice given by the Boss and Ganesh work? What if it did not? What should he do then? What if these black figures did not get scared of him? What if they still insisted on climbing over? What would he do then? And what if they actually decided to confront him instead of running away? What if they were not just stupid teenagers as he had been told? What then? How would he find the courage to confront them if at all it got to that stage? He did not have the answers to all those questions.

But for some reason that did not affect his confidence. He was ready to get reckless for another train of thought ran quickly through his mind. What if they did get scared and run away? What if he succeeded in intimidating them? What if they never showed up again and left the garden alone? That would be great, he answered. Truly great. That would be a decisive victory for him, a confidence booster.

And that positive train of thought was more overpowering and more inspiring than the first negative train of thought. And that positive thought propelled him into action for the sweet thought of victory was much more alluring than the bitter thought of defeat.

And so he ran out toward them with all his newfound confidence and positivity and thoughts of victory and with the powerful torch directed at them and the thick stick aggressively hitting the ground, shouting in a vicious voice, "Get out of here! All of you! Get out of here right now!"

The black figures were all paralyzed with fear. The three figures who were helping the two bulky figures climb up backed away from the gate in panic and stood there looking into the darkness beyond the gate trying to figure out whom did the voice belong to.

One of the bulky figures who had almost reached the top of the gate was so struck with fear that he fell down to the ground. Then he got up in a hurry and ran over to the other three a little away from the gate.

The other bulky figure was exactly at the top of the gate sitting in the middle with each leg on either side of the gate. He panicked on hearing the vicious voice and in that moment he was confused as to which side he should jump and run. He could not decide in that state of panic and so he remained sitting there on the top of the gate.

Now the four of them that were on the ground stared through the gate into the garden, their hearts thumping and their mouths trembling. And all they could see was a powerful beam of light moving in the dark toward the gate. The powerful light hit their eyes, blinding them and making them flinch. And they could hear the hitting of the stick against the ground and a voice shouting, "Get out of here! All of you!"

And so, terribly frightened, they obeyed the voice and ran away leaving the solitary bulky figure on the top of the gate.

Aryan saw the four of them running away. He grinned. But he continued the shouting and hitting and flashing for the last bulky figure still sat there on the top utterly confused and frightened and lost.

Aryan shouted at him, "Hey you! What are you waiting for? Should I call the police?"

He saw the bulky boy trembling up there with his eyes away from the glare of the dangerous torch. The boy was about to cry and Aryan noticed that. He stopped shouting now but he continued to torture the boy with the torch and the stick.

The boy could not move due to fear and he struggled to say something but his voice did not support him. It looked as if his voice had run away along with the others. Aryan felt bad now. He relaxed a bit but kept up his guard. He lowered the torch from the boy's face and pointed it at his stomach.

The boy felt the heat of the light shift from his face to his stomach. He knew now that he could see again. He blinked his eyes rapidly a few times and then he turned his head around slowly and cautiously and looked at Aryan.

Aryan was still hitting the stick on the ground. He waited for a response or some movement. He was alert. The boy was his enemy for now and he could not let his guard down yet even though the boy looked quite harmless.

The light of the torch was so powerful that it perfectly illuminated the boy's face without hurting his eyes. The boy's face was dark and chubby and his eyes red and frightened. He looked like a teenager.

"What do you want?" Aryan shouted. "You want me to hit you with this stick?"

Aryan laughed in his mind when he heard himself say that. He was talking like a gangster, he thought. And he was enjoying it too. It was the power of the stick. It was intoxicating.

The boy said nothing. He looked at Aryan with wide eyes, his body trembling. He could not believe what was happening to him. He looked at the other side again and he saw no one. All his friends had run away and escaped and they had left him all alone.

"Can't you speak?" Aryan asked him. "Are you dumb?"

The boy shook his head but said nothing. He continued to stare at Aryan.

"Do you know what will happen if I hit you with this stick?" Aryan said, pointing the stick at the helpless boy.

The boy shook his head again.

"It will break your bones," said Aryan.

Aryan looked at him with a serious expression. He wanted to convey to the boy that he was not messing around and that he was serious. And it seemed to be working. The boy nodded at him, indicating that he understood the threat perfectly well.

"What did you come here for?" Aryan asked him. "To do what?"

The boy said nothing. He swallowed his spit. Then he shook his head slowly.

"So what do you want to do?" Aryan asked him. "Jump on this side and enter the garden so that I can smack you with this stick?"

The boy shook his head again.

"Or do you want to jump on the other side and run away like your friends?"

The boy nodded rapidly. He wished to opt for the second option.

"Good," Aryan said with authority. "Get down slowly now and run away and never come back. And tell that to your friends too. Never come back to this garden. You understand?"

The boy nodded again.

"Good," Aryan said. "Get out of here now before I break your legs with this stick."

The boy quickly turned and brought his leg

to the other side of the gate. Then without thinking or preparing he jumped straight down from the top of the gate and landed on the ground horizontally. Then he got up with great difficulty and limped away in the direction in which his friends had gone. He did not look back.

A satisfied smile came over Aryan's face. He was proud of himself. His chest swelled up and his shoulders fell back. His spine straightened up. He was grinning now with confidence. Victory was his, he said to himself. The risk had paid off. He was convinced now that he could be intimidating enough. He would do well at this job, he thought. He had done his duty well for now.

But the thing that excited him the most was the thrill of the confrontation. The adrenaline rush that he had felt before he was about to confront them was something that could not be described in words, he thought. No matter what would have been the result of the confrontation, defeat or victory, the rush that he had felt surging within him was worth it.

He wondered if he was making too much out of it. After all there had been no real confrontation. Not even close. But the knowledge that he had the ability to strike fear into another person's heart and that he could frighten and intimidate them was very satisfying to have. It was pleasing to his ego.

No wonder people craved for power, he thought and smiled. It did make sense. Power made one feel invincible. It made one feel immortal. It made one feel that one could never get hurt and that no one could ever harm one. It was dangerous, he said to himself, for it was intoxicating.

Aryan went back into the cabin and sat down on the chair. He kept the stick standing against the wall and he kept the torch on his lap. He picked up the bottle of water and drank from it. It was a long sip. Then he kept the bottle down on the floor and raised his feet up and kept them on the stool. He folded his hands behind his head and grinned again.

He started thinking now. If such a small incident could produce such an intense reaction within him he wondered what an actual confrontation would produce. No wonder some people loved confrontations, he thought. No wonder people liked to intimidate others. No wonder people were proud of themselves when they instilled fear in others.

It was all about feeling powerful. Power was the most powerful drug. And craving for power was a dangerous tendency inherent in all human beings. It was a terrible tendency, he said to himself. He must beware of it for it could turn him into something he was not or maybe into something he truly was.

Then again, as always, he ridiculed himself for making such a big deal out of it. It was so stupid of him, he told himself. Why did he do that? he asked himself. When had he acquired this silly habit? He did not know. But he wanted to stop it. He wanted to stop making a big deal out of every minor occurrence.

He felt better after ridiculing himself. He felt sane again. He searched for the clock on the wall. It was only one thirty-five. Barely five minutes had passed since he first saw the five figures at the gate. So weird, he said to himself. It had seemed to him as if the incident had lasted for at least twenty minutes.

He smiled. He felt his head getting heavy again and his eyelids shutting on their own. He closed his eyes to save himself from the effort of keeping them open and fell asleep immediately.

CHAPTER 8

Aryan waited and watched for much longer than he had expected.

Five days went by and not a single painting had been sold. He was disappointed and demotivated now. People who walked by his stall stood and stared at his paintings in wonder and they all commented with generosity on each one's beauty. But no one was willing to buy them. Not for five hundred rupees at least. They preferred to just stand and admire and comment on them from afar.

After five days he was convinced it was a bad idea. It had become quite clear to him that no one was really interested in buying his paintings. Maybe they were not good enough, he thought. He did not want to take them back home now and so he decided to give them all away for free to anyone who would care to ask for them. He did not care anymore. He just wanted to get rid of them.

He cut out a small square piece of cardboard and he wrote on it carelessly, 'Free Paintings.' Then he stuck it to the table. He was still uncertain whether people would ask for his paintings even if they were given away for free. Once again all he could do was wait and watch.

On the night of the fifth day, after selling his catch, he started packing up his things to leave for home. Three paintings were still displayed on the table and the other three were still at the foot of the table with just one lamp throwing a little light on them.

The small cardboard sign saying, 'Free Paintings,' was casually taped to the table. Just before he could finish packing he heard a deep voice address him.

"Hello there, young man. Are these your paintings?" the voice said.

Aryan turned around to see whom the voice belonged to. He saw a tall slim man who was smartly dressed. The man was wearing a dark-blue shirt and black trousers. His black shoes were polished and shining. His hair was combed sideways and he had a thin patchy beard on his thin oval face. The little light provided by the lamp on the ground was enough to see that the man looked completely out of place. Aryan had never seen such a well-dressed man in the market before. He wondered if the gentleman was lost.

"Yes, they are," replied Aryan. "I'm giving them away for free. Would you be interested?"

"Really?" the man asked. "You are willing to give away such beautiful paintings for free? And why would you do that?"

The man seemed genuinely confused.

"I tried selling them for five hundred rupees each but no one was willing to pay that much. And now I'm fed up. I just want to get rid of them."

"Five hundred rupees?" said the man. "That's all you asked for these paintings? My God, you really underestimate your talent, young man."

He was amused by Aryan's foolishness.

"What's your name?" the man asked.

"Aryan."

"Well, Aryan, do you know that your paintings would sell for thousands in Mumbai? Maybe even more. That's where I come from. I live in Mumbai and trust me I know the value of such paintings. There are rich people who even pay lakhs for paintings that are not even half as good as your paintings. You have the potential to become a successful artist if you are willing to come to Mumbai and start your career. You can even become rich."

The man smiled. Aryan looked at him carefully with suspicious eyes to try and figure out if he was serious or joking. The man stared back at him with the same smile still on his face. Aryan could not figure it out.

"Thousands? Lakhs? For these paintings? What are you even talking about, sir?"

"Trust me," said the man. "You have the skill and talent for it. You are wasting away your talent in this fish market, young man. You are destined for greater things."

Aryan said nothing. He stared at the man

and started thinking. Was he really destined for greater things? he wondered.

"Anyway, here's my card," the man said, giving his card. "In case you decide to come to Mumbai give me a call. Also I would like to buy two of your paintings. And I would like to pay for them."

Aryan was surprised to hear the man say that and quickly sat up straight.

"Which ones did you like?" Aryan asked him.

"I like that peacock painting and that portrait of the fisherwoman right there," the man said, pointing at the respective paintings.

Aryan handed over the two paintings to the man.

"You can pay me whatever you feel like. I don't know how much they may be worth. You seem to know better."

"I shall pay you one thousand rupees for each," said the man. "Here's two thousand for both."

Aryan was shocked. He could not believe his luck. He stared at the cash in the man's hand.

"Two thousand? Are you sure?" Aryan asked.

"Of course I am," the man said with a smile. "You deserve it. Maybe you can use it to come to Mumbai."

"Thank you so much," Aryan said and stretched out his hand hesitatingly to take the cash. "Sorry I forgot to ask you your name."

"Vincent," the man replied. "It's on the card."

"Thank you, Vincent."

"Hope we meet again someday," Vincent said

and walked away into the surrounding darkness.

That night on reaching home Aryan told his mother everything that had happened to him. He told her about the meeting with Vincent and how he had tried to persuade him to come to Mumbai to become an artist. And most importantly he told her about how Vincent had paid him two thousand rupees for two paintings like it was nothing at all. She was shocked when she heard the amount.

"Seems like he was a very rich man," she said. "I heard Mumbai is full of rich people. Maybe he's one of them."

"Maybe. I just know that his name is Vincent and that he's a businessman," he said, and then he took out the card that Vincent had given him.

"Look here Ma, he gave me his card and told me to call him if I ever decided to go to Mumbai."

She looked at the card and smiled. She did not know how to read.

"He seems like a nice man," she said and went to the kitchen.

He did not continue the conversation. He waited for her to bring up the subject of him going to Mumbai. But she did not. He waited for some more time and then after a few minutes of silence when he noticed that she had no intention of bringing it up he decided to do it himself.

"So what do you think, Ma?" he asked, trying to be as casual as possible.

"What do I think about what?" she said.

"About me going to Mumbai."

She turned around and looked at him.

"You took that man seriously?" she asked.

He did not respond. He was looking at the address written on Vincent's card. He kept on concentrating on the word Mumbai. Suddenly that word which he had heard so many times before became irresistibly attractive and appealing to him.

"I don't know," he said. "It just got me thinking again. I feel that I'm wasting away my life over here. I feel I can go on to do bigger things in life. And if what Vincent says is true then maybe it won't be as impossible as I had imagined. He said that I may even become rich. I don't know, Ma. I'm confused. But I'm sure that if I don't give it a try now I will regret it for the rest of my life. I will curse myself every day for not having the courage to chase my dream. I know it's selfish of me. I'm aware of it. But I still feel I need to do something about it at least once."

He stopped talking. She stood there looking at her son. She understood him. She felt his pain and his anguish. She could see the frustration on his face. He was restless for a new life and she could see it. She just could not do it to him. She knew she could not. She could not deny him his dream for she knew it would be unfair to him. She knew he was living a life he truly detested and she just could not deny him his chance, probably his only chance.

Then she said in a soft voice, "Do you really feel

that way?"

He did not answer. She went to the cupboard and opened it. She took out a purple cloth which was carefully kept hidden under a few clothes and then she came back to Aryan.

"Here," she said, untying the purple cloth. There was money inside it. "It's not much but it will help you to survive for some time in Mumbai."

There were four thousand rupees in it. He had no idea when and how she had managed to save so much. He refrained from asking her.

"You can keep it along with the two thousand you earned tonight," she said, smiling. "You will have enough to travel to Mumbai and maybe find some accommodation until you start earning as an artist."

She smiled at him but he did not smile back. He just stared at her with a sad expression on his face.

"But how will you manage?" he asked.

"You don't worry about all that. I have saved some more," she lied. "And besides, we have very helpful neighbors who would help me in a heartbeat. You just focus on making your dream come true and make me proud."

He nodded. Then he walked up to her and embraced her.

CHAPTER 9

Aryan slept till four in the morning. He only woke up now because he felt the urge to urinate. He took the torch in his hand and stood up. He looked at the clock and saw the time. He realized he had slept for almost two and a half hours.

He was still sleepy and his eyes barely opened up. His head was aching. Mosquitoes roamed about his feet and he tried to kick them away. But they returned. They always returned.

He shook his head. He walked out of the cabin and switched on the torch and then he walked over to the toilet near his shed. He relieved himself while holding the torch under his armpit.

He could literally relieve himself anywhere in the garden, he thought. Who would know about it? No one. Who would care about it? No one. He smiled. And anyway, he thought, the trees and plants were all dried up here. They desperately needed some watering. He stopped thinking. Then he laughed at his thought.

When he came out of the toilet he was still half-asleep. The shed was calling to him to come in and sleep on the comfortable mattress. He stopped in front of the shed door. Who would even find out he slept in there? he wondered. No one would. Absolutely no one. But what if he overslept? What if he overslept and then Ganesh would catch him sleeping there in the morning? That would not be good, he told himself. No, not at all.

He walked on to the cabin and settled down on the chair again. It was still dark everywhere except for the orange street lights outside. There was silence. There were mosquitoes. There were the sounds of insects. Occasionally a vehicle would pass by the gate almost in a flash. And then there would be nothing else for a long time.

He stared at the gate for almost half an hour. He saw no movement at all. No one was there. It was too late for anyone to come now, he thought. Even jobless delinquents slept at this hour. He managed to stay awake till five and then he fell asleep again.

At seven Ganesh entered the cabin and shook Aryan by the shoulder. Aryan did not get up. Ganesh shook him harder and said, "Get up! Quick! The boss is here!"

Aryan heard it as if he had heard it in a dream and he suddenly sat up straight like a dead man waking up. Then he stood up and looked hard at Ganesh's face with his slightly opened eyes. His vision was blurry. He started rubbing his eyes with his finger. Slowly his vision cleared up and he saw Ganesh's face clearly. Ganesh was smiling at him.

"Good morning," said Ganesh. "I see you are

hard at your duty."

Aryan looked down, ashamed. He rubbed his eyes again. He chose not to respond.

"You were so fast asleep that I had no choice but to say that the boss was here," Ganesh said with a mischievous smile.

"I'm sorry," Aryan said. "I'm not used to it. It's difficult to stay up like this."

"I would never be able to do it."

"So the boss won't know?" Aryan asked.

"Who would tell him?" asked Ganesh, smiling. "And he wouldn't care anyway. Do you want tea? There's a tea stall outside barely two minutes away."

"I would love some tea," Aryan said.

Ganesh kept his plastic bag on the floor of the cabin and then the two of them opened the side gate and walked out, closing it behind them but not locking it. Then they turned right and walked toward the tea stall.

While walking Aryan asked Ganesh, "How did you enter the garden?"

"I climbed over," Ganesh said. "What else could I do?"

They both laughed. They reached the tea stall and asked for two small cups of ginger tea. The man behind the counter handed them two small glasses with the tea occupying only half the glass. The tea was hot and they blew into it. They waited for a few seconds before they started drinking it. Then they drank in silence. They looked around.

The sun was up but the air was still cool. Soon it would get warmer. No sunlight fell on the road or the trees yet. It was a pleasant hour.

The road was busy with a few vehicles now. There were four other men standing and drinking tea around the stall. They all looked like they were on their way to work, all dressed up sharply in formals and with bags on their shoulders.

Aryan's head felt heavy. He had a slightly uncomfortable feeling within him but he could not describe what it was. Maybe it was the sleep, he said to himself while sipping his tea. The only thing worse than not sleeping at all was drifting in and out of sleep. Disturbed sleep was always frustrating. It messed with one's head and body. Either one must not sleep at all or sleep properly, he told himself.

They finished their tea and kept their glasses on the counter. The man behind the counter quickly took them away. Ganesh paid for both of them and then they started walking back.

While walking back Aryan narrated the entire incident to Ganesh. Ganesh listened to him with great interest. They reached the gate of the garden and swung it open and entered in and then locked it.

Ganesh went into the cabin and Aryan walked over to the shed taking small lazy steps. He entered the shed and laid out the mattress immediately. He changed out of his uniform and folded it and kept it on the floor next to the wall. He changed into a pair of shorts and a t-shirt.

He would have a bath and eat something after waking up, he decided. This was going to be his daily routine now and he was prepared for it. His life had officially changed. Very soon he would turn into a nocturnal creature.

He lay down on the mattress, using his folded arm as a pillow, and he fell asleep almost instantly.

CHAPTER 10

Aryan boarded an early morning train to Mumbai from Kornur station.

It was the first time he was traveling outside of Kornur and he had been extremely anxious about it from the start. His mother had accompanied him to the station to wish him goodbye and both mother and son had shed tears on that lonely and empty platform just before he boarded the train.

He traveled with a heart that was heavy with sadness and hope and guilt. But his mind was finally set free for the first time in many years. It had suddenly gained its freedom and it was free at last to dream, to dream again and again.

The train arrived in Mumbai after a twenty-hour journey. He was tired and sleep-deprived but he was glad he had finally arrived in Mumbai, a place he had imagined a hundred times over just by looking at Vincent's card.

He looked out of his window and saw hundreds of people walking about in all directions. His anxiety soared. They all seemed to be in a great hurry as if they would miss something terribly important if they happened to be late.

He had never seen such a crowd at any station before. At Kornur station there had been barely anyone at all on the platform, but here even before he could get down from the train he felt completely lost just by witnessing this huge fast-moving crowd from his window. He was alone and he felt lonely. He was afraid.

He got down from the train and looked around for the exit. Then he started walking toward it without having any clue as to where it was. He found it quite difficult and confusing to navigate the platforms and bridges through that immense sea of men and women and children and he asked random people for directions every other minute in his broken Hindi.

He was nervous as this was his first trip outside of Kornur. And in a city like Mumbai even someone who has lived in it for their entire life can feel hopelessly lost at times.

Eventually he found his way outside the station where he faced, yet again, hundreds of people walking and running and shouting and going about their daily activities. With great difficulty he managed to find a rickshaw and then he asked the driver in his broken Hindi to take him to a cheap hotel.

He had just about six thousand rupees with him. He thought it would be more than enough until he could start earning properly by selling his paintings.

The driver took him to a hotel where he could

find accommodation for a few days but the rooms seemed to be quite expensive. He could not afford it. So he asked the driver to take him to a cheaper hotel. The driver reluctantly asked a few questions to a shopkeeper of which Aryan understood enough to know that the driver was asking for another cheaper hotel nearby.

After twenty minutes of going through narrow crowded lanes and dodging dogs and cows and vehicles and people the driver stopped in front of a shady motel that looked old and worn-down. The name of the motel was Paradise Motel. Aryan inquired about the rates and found out he could afford it for now. His plan was to settle down in his room and then give Vincent a call immediately.

After he set down his luggage in his room he had a quick cold bath. He felt refreshed now. Then he went down to the reception and called Vincent. But Vincent did not pick up his call. He panicked. The only reason he had decided to come to Mumbai was because he had believed in what Vincent had told him. He thought Vincent would help him get in touch with a few people in the art industry.

He was panicking much too quickly for within a minute Vincent called back on the reception line and the receptionist picked up the call and handed it over to Aryan.

At first Vincent did not recognize Aryan's name or voice which led Aryan to panic again. Then Aryan reminded Vincent of their meeting in Kornur and Vincent immediately remembered him. He apologized to Aryan.

Aryan felt relieved. He told Vincent he was in Mumbai now, that he had finally made it. Vincent did not believe him at first but once he was convinced he was glad that Aryan was in Mumbai. He asked Aryan about his mother. How would she manage without him? Vincent wanted to know. Aryan told him he would explain everything to him later on when they would meet.

The two of them decided to meet by six that evening near Paradise Motel so that Aryan would not have to travel anywhere. After their talk Aryan slept for a few hours. And he slept peacefully. He got up by five in order to get ready for his meeting with Vincent. He felt relaxed. All his fears of being in a new city had completely vanished for now. He was confident and optimistic.

By six Aryan and Vincent met at a restaurant close to Paradise Motel in order to catch up. They greeted each other warmly and with familiarity and then they settled down at a small compact table and ordered two cups of ginger tea. They got comfortable and they began to talk.

Vincent was curious to know how Aryan had changed his mind so quickly. Aryan told him about the discussion that he had had with his mother the very night that Vincent had met him. He explained in detail how he had acquired the money to come to Mumbai and to sustain himself for some time until he would start earning. Vincent was glad.

"But I must warn you it won't be that easy," said Vincent. "You will have to struggle and persevere in order to succeed."

"I know," Aryan said.

"I will introduce you to a friend of mine named Rashid. He runs an art gallery here. If he happens to like your paintings he will readily display them in his gallery."

Aryan nodded and thanked Vincent for the opportunity. He was grateful to Vincent.

Then the two of them fell into general chatting while they ate their respective masala dosas. By seven-thirty they were done with their little meeting. Vincent invited Aryan for dinner at his home but Aryan refused.

"I have eaten enough for the day," Aryan said with great satisfaction. "I won't be hungry for dinner."

"Are you sure?" Vincent asked.

"Very sure," Aryan said.

They shook each other's hand and said goodbye to each other. Then they dispersed. Aryan walked back to his motel and went straight up to his room. He was tired and still sleep-deprived. He quickly removed his sandals and changed his clothes and then he went to bed.

CHAPTER 11

Aryan had still not received any news regarding the sale of his paintings. A year had gone by since he had started working at the garden and Rashid had not contacted him even once during that time.

And so he rightly assumed that his paintings had not been sold. The false hope that he had had at first had vanished away completely. In fact he did not even remember exactly how his paintings looked.

They were probably taken down long ago, he told himself again and again. If they had been sold Vincent would have informed him about it when they met on Sundays. And he saw no point in contacting Rashid now as he believed it was too late to do that.

On certain rare occasions when he would remember about his paintings he would ask Vincent if he had heard anything from Rashid and Vincent would always reply in the negative. Finally one day, around six months into the job, Aryan gave up for good. He had not felt much sadness or regret about it and he himself was surprised by the manner in which he had reacted to such a decision.

He just did not think about it much anymore. Time had numbed his feelings toward it like it did toward everything.

Aryan was fairly content with his life although it was a huge step down from what he had imagined for himself. A year ago he had hoped his paintings would be sold by now. And he had hoped to start painting again by now. But neither of those things had happened. He had made no progress at all in that direction. But nonetheless he was trudging on.

Within those twelve long months Aryan had realized that the course of his life would not be dictated by him. Who would dictate it? He did not know. And he did not care. Maybe the mysterious laws of nature would dictate it, he thought, or maybe life itself. But he knew for certain that it was not in his hands. He could only do certain things within his limits. As for the rest, life itself would decide on it, not him. Life would take its own course and he had to just ride along with it without complaining. All he had to do was accept that absurd fact. And he did exactly that. And then he was at peace.

It was oddly comforting to him. Knowing and accepting that fact forced him to take life less seriously now. He was not as important, he had realized. No one was. Human beings were mere toys, helpless creatures, just like all other creatures. We were in no way special at all. We were like insects. Nothing was in our hands. Life could do with us as it pleased. It could protect us or it could destroy us in an instant. And we could do absolutely nothing about it but accept it. That was its will and we were subject to it just like all the other creatures were.

Vincent was against it but Aryan insisted on it. He said he had stumbled upon this fact while on duty, while he was contemplating in that silence, while he was surrounded by that darkness, while he was killing mosquitoes, while he was asleep and dreaming.

They spoke about this one Sunday afternoon while eating lunch and Vincent had wondered what had happened to Aryan.

"So you have lost all ambition?" Vincent had asked Aryan.

"I never said that," Aryan had said.

"Then what is all this talk about?" Vincent said. "You sound like you have been brainwashed."

Aryan laughed. Then he said, "Maybe I was. But I did it to myself."

"You can't let go of your dreams like this," Vincent said. "Blaming life for everything is just the easy way out. You must take responsibility."

"But don't you agree even a little?" said Aryan. "Don't you agree that things are not always in our hands?"

"Not always," Vincent said. "But they are in our hands more than enough. And blaming Life or God or Nature or the Universe is just silly talk."

"I don't blame anything," Aryan said. "All I'm

saying is it will happen when it will happen. And it will happen at the right time."

"It will happen when you make it happen," Vincent said. "Sometimes there's no right time. The right time is whenever you choose it to be. Sounds to me like you are making excuses."

Aryan remained silent. It did sound like that, he agreed. He thought about it but found no answer. He knew he was right in what he thought. But he could not deny the fact that Vincent was right too from his point of view. He was a flawed philosopher, he teased himself.

"I told you I can help you out," Vincent had said. "I can still do it."

"Not this again," Aryan said, smiling.

"Don't move in. And don't leave your job. But at least continue painting. I will help you."

"I must help myself," Aryan said and then changed the subject.

They never discussed the matter again.

CHAPTER 12

Aryan and Vincent went together in Vincent's car to meet Rashid in his art gallery. Aryan was both excited and nervous, and Vincent tried to calm him down.

Aryan knew he had some good paintings to show but he was not sure whether Rashid would like them or not. After all art had always been subjective in nature.

They entered a posh gallery that had a top floor too and they saw beautiful paintings displayed on the walls. The thought of possibly having one of his paintings displayed up on these walls someday excited Aryan to such an extent that he could not conceal his wide smile as he walked about the gallery, completely lost and transfixed. And then he heard Vincent call out in the opposite direction, "Rashid!"

He turned around to see in the direction in which Vincent had called out and saw Rashid for the first time. He was a short man with a perfectly round face and he was wearing round spectacles to go with it. He had a bald head and he looked old, maybe in his early sixties, but he had a kind of youthfulness in his step. He looked quite energetic for his age. He was a heavy-set man, and he was dressed in a white shirt and black trousers and a red tie and a black coat.

Aryan was also in his best clothes in order to make a good impression, but his best clothes just happened to be a brown pant that had been recently ironed and a black half-sleeve shirt that he had neatly tucked into his pants. And he was wearing an old worn-out pair of sandals. This was the best he could do.

Vincent introduced them to each other. Rashid and Aryan greeted each other formally and then Aryan went on to explain his purpose for coming to meet Rashid. Rashid listened to him carefully, with patience, even though he knew precisely the reason for Aryan's visit for Vincent had already informed him over the phone.

Then Rashid led them into his office on the first floor. After completing all petty formalities of decency he asked them if they would like to have some tea and begin the discussion. They replied that they would like that very much.

As they waited for their tea to arrive Rashid asked Aryan if he could see the paintings now.

Aryan carefully opened up the ragged brown cloth bag in which he was carrying his carefully-packed paintings. Since they were not that big in size he was able to carry them around with just a little difficulty.

There were five paintings, none of them

properly framed, and Aryan laid them out on the table in front of him. Rashid examined the paintings for a few minutes, and for those few minutes there was complete silence.

Rashid was impressed, and he noticed Aryan's obvious talent. No one could deny it. But he felt like something vital was amiss.

"You clearly have amazing skill and technique," said Rashid. "It's obvious, I can't deny it. These paintings are beautiful, but they lack innovation. They lack an out-of-the-box idea. You understand?"

Aryan did not. He looked at Rashid blankly. He was perplexed.

"Well, let me put it this way," Rashid said. "Your paintings are wonderful pieces of realistic art. They look like some photographs taken. And you have amazing technique. No doubt. But nowadays people are more obsessed with something wild and more spontaneous. Something beyond a realistic painting. Something like Picasso or Dali's paintings. You see now?"

Aryan was even more confused now. He did not understand what Rashid had meant by something wild nor did he know who Picasso or Dali was. He looked at Vincent and then at Rashid and then he looked down at his sweaty palms. He wiped them on his pants.

Rashid sensed his confusion and decided to show him what he had meant. He took Aryan on a tour of the gallery, showing him various kinds of abstract paintings in the guise of surrealist and cubist and fauvist paintings, which were all anything but realistic.

Why would anyone spend their money on such abnormal paintings that had no realistic element in them? Aryan wondered. But he could do that too, he thought. He would learn to paint in such a way if that was what was required of him.

He asked Rashid to give him a chance. He could do it, he said. It was possible. He promised to make something much better than the paintings displayed there and he said that it would be wilder and more innovative and more creative than anything ever seen before.

Rashid was taken aback by his confidence and so was Vincent. They looked at each other and smiled. They were genuinely impressed by his attitude and Rashid decided to give him a chance and also agreed to display three of his paintings in the gallery.

"Maybe someone's still interested in a beautiful piece of realistic art," said Rashid. "If they are, your paintings will surely sell."

Aryan could not be more grateful. Not only had Rashid given him a chance to learn and create something new but he had also accepted three of his paintings to display them. If they were sold, Aryan would get sixty percent of the proceeds, Rashid said.

Aryan did not reply. He looked at Vincent for some guidance as he was extremely ignorant in such matters. Vincent looked back at him and wondered why he was not responding. Then on understanding his problem Vincent turned to Rashid and smiled and said, "Great! Sounds good."

Rashid smiled back. Then he put out his hand to Vincent and said, "Alright then. Deal."

"Deal," Vincent said and shook his hand.

Then Rashid turned to Aryan with the same smile still on his face and put out his hand to him and said, "Deal."

"Deal," said Aryan, shaking his hand.

And then Aryan and Vincent left the gallery and walked toward Vincent's car. Aryan was a happy man with a new-found determination. He relished the new challenge.

They reached Vincent's car and stopped. They spoke for a few minutes and then Aryan thanked Vincent and left for the motel on foot and Vincent left for his office. As Aryan walked back to the motel he had a feeling that his life was about to change.

CHAPTER 13

A week after starting with the job Aryan's routine had been fixed. He had really struggled for that first week, but after that, once he got used to staying awake at night and sleeping in the morning, it was smooth sailing. And now, a year later, he was comfortable with it.

The delinquents had now completely stopped trying to enter the garden. They tried to climb over every other day during the first month but were repelled by Aryan each time. During the second month they tried to climb over every third day but were successfully chased away by Aryan. During the third month they tried to climb over twice a week at least but they failed each time. During the fourth month they tried to enter in once a week but Aryan sent them running away every time. Finally, from the fifth month onwards, they stopped trying altogether.

Occasionally, once a month or so, some other bunch of teenage delinquents who were totally unaware of Aryan's presence there tried in vain to jump over the gate. But they never succeeded at it and instead ended up receiving the shock of their lives.

These sporadic visits finally stopped completely around the eighth month, and word had spread quickly on the streets among the scared teenage community that a big scary man with a long thick stick and a blinding torch and an insane mind lived in that garden and protected it. A lot of the details were blatantly exaggerated for they were teenagers after all.

No one knew whether he was the watchman or whether he was just living there. Some believed he was a ghost. Some said that he was a crazy man, very strong and totally insane, who lived there thinking it was his home. No one knew the truth and no one dared to find out.

But all were afraid now. No one visited the garden anymore. It was no longer an option for delinquents if they wanted to live, so the word spread. No smoking or drinking or intake of drugs took place there now. The mission had been accomplished. The boss was right, Aryan had thought. They were really dumb teenagers, scared and guilt-ridden. The job had been easy.

From the ninth month onwards no one ever dared to visit the abandoned garden. Aryan was left completely free with all the time in the world at his disposal. He had the whole dark silent night to himself every day and he used it to think and wonder and dream. He introspected. He questioned himself. He questioned the world. He grudgingly philosophized for he could not help it.

It was his natural disposition to do so whenever in the midst of silence and boredom and darkness.

And he tried to find out all the answers by himself for he had no one to talk to. He had slowly befriended the tea vendor, Bittu, where he went to drink tea at least thrice in the night while on duty and once in the morning with Ganesh.

But Bittu was not someone Aryan could talk to about such things. Aryan knew that very well. He had tried it once before and had soon realized that Bittu did not care about such stuff. Bittu's entire life revolved around the tea stall and cricket and movies. That was all and nothing more.

Bittu did not worry about pointless questions on life and God and religion and mosquitoes. That was not him. He was normal, unlike Aryan. Normal people did not think about such superfluous stuff. They did not like to waste their time thinking about things that had no definite answers or solutions. And they were absolutely right. Why should they? Why should anyone? Aryan wondered.

Normal people did not have the time or patience to do that. They had to work and earn and survive and live. They did not have empty hours to fill as he did. They had other bigger responsibilities, other important stuff. They had family and friends. They had concerns and worries of their own.

So why would they worry about the world at large? Why would they think about the purpose of life? Why would they bother questioning the existence of God? Why would they take the trouble to question or criticize any religion? Why? Aryan wondered.

The answer was quite obvious to him. Normal people did not do all that because it was not worth it. Not even a bit. If anything, it was troublesome and tiresome. It was a burden to think about all that. It simply complicated life, making it more difficult. It was better to not question things and go with the flow than to question things and go against it. It was better to be a part of the status quo than to stand isolated and alone. It was safer to submit to tradition, submit to a religion, submit to a God, than to challenge them all. For one would always lose if they did so, or at least that was what everyone believed.

And so Aryan did not blame Bittu for not caring about such unnecessary things that did not help anyone nor make their lives easier or happier in any way. And Bittu was young too, only seventeen years old. It was not Bittu's fault that he preferred to talk about cricket or movies for that was what normal people did.

And Bittu was normal. It was he who was at fault, Aryan realized. It was he who was abnormal. He was the one who was in the wrong for questioning or thinking about such things. Things that could not be questioned or thought of but must only be blindly accepted.

And so Aryan only spoke to Bittu about cricket

and movies every single time. And on very rare occasions Aryan would tell Bittu about Kornur and his life over there. And in return Bittu would tell Aryan about his family's history and about how his father had come to start this tea stall fifteen years ago. In this way within a year they had become very good friends.

CHAPTER 14

The very next day Vincent and Aryan got to work. Vincent sponsored Aryan with the money to buy whatever he required.

The two of them traveled around the city in Vincent's car, searching for the right shop that would provide Aryan with all his needs, and they finally found one in the suburbs that they were happy with. They bought canvases, paints, paintbrushes, a palette, and other little things that would be required by him.

Vincent spent a good amount on them, and he did it generously without any hesitation or regret. Aryan was grateful to him and he said so. Vincent jokingly asked Aryan to pay him back once he became a famous artist. Aryan laughed and said he would.

It was almost eight at night by the time they were done with their shopping. Both of them were hungry and they decided to go to a Chinese restaurant to have their dinner. They sat in the air-conditioned room at a table for two and they asked for a menu. A waiter came and handed it over to Aryan. They began to talk and browse through it.

Now that the tools for painting were all acquired the question arose as to where Aryan would paint. He could not paint in his motel room for long as he would soon run out of money. He needed someplace more permanent where he ran no risk of being kicked out anytime soon. Vincent invited him to move into his house but Aryan was not so sure.

"I don't want to be a burden on you," he said. "You have already done enough for me."

"There's no question of you being a burden at all," Vincent said. "Anyway I live alone. And I have three rooms out of which I really use just one. You can use one of the rooms as your studio."

Aryan did not say anything. He concentrated on the menu, struggling to find anything he liked. Every dish on the menu was completely unknown to him. He had never even heard of them. He closed the menu and passed it over to Vincent and said, "I can't understand anything."

Vincent looked at the menu and within thirty short seconds he decided what they would have. He summoned the waiter over to their table and said, "One plate Chicken Triple Schezwan Rice and one plate Chicken Crispy."

The waiter nodded at him and repeated the order twice. He did not care to write it down. He asked them if they needed anything else. Vincent said they did not for now. If they did, they would let him know, he told the waiter. The waiter smiled and went away.

"Don't you have Chinese food in Kornur?" Vincent asked.

"No," Aryan said. "We don't have such fancy restaurants there. Just roadside stuff. But mostly we eat only homemade food."

"That's good. So what do you think?"

"About what?"

"About staying with me," Vincent said. "I don't see any other option."

"Me neither," Aryan said and looked down at the table. He hesitated to say anything further.

Vincent looked at him from across the table. He waited for Aryan to continue. Aryan did not. He was still hesitant.

"You won't be any burden, you know," Vincent said.

"I think you are right," Aryan said. "But you have done enough for me."

"That's it, you are moving in with me tomorrow," Vincent said. He knew Aryan was as good as convinced. He was right.

"Okay," Aryan said with a smile.

He wondered how anyone could be as nice as Vincent. He was a rare human being, Aryan thought.

Their order finally arrived and they began to eat hurriedly as if their food were about to run away. The food was terribly hot but they did not care. They were too hungry and they hogged it all down their throats. They called for more water and then for some lemon juice. And then they were overfull and uncomfortable but perfectly satisfied. They struggled to walk toward the car. They walked slowly and unsteadily and they entered in and sank into their seats.

"Did you like it?" Vincent asked after two minutes of silence.

"I loved it," Aryan said and laughed.

Vincent joined him and they laughed together for a few seconds. Then Vincent started the car and they drove away.

The next day Aryan moved out of the Paradise Motel and moved into Vincent's apartment. He had just one suitcase along with him and all his painting tools were already in Vincent's apartment. Vincent showed Aryan his spare room in which Aryan could sleep as well as paint. Aryan was amazed by Vincent's posh flat and he looked around in wonder. It must be quite expensive, he thought, but he did not say it out loud.

"What do you do for a living, Vincent?" Aryan asked casually.

"I'm just a small-time businessman dealing in real estate, that's all," said Vincent.

Aryan settled down in the flat and then he set up all his painting apparatus in the room. Vincent gave him strict instructions to consider the flat as his own home and Aryan agreed and said that he would gladly do so.

Aryan had decided to start painting from the next day onwards.

CHAPTER 15

The one thing that had not changed at all in Aryan's daily routine was his afternoon walks. In the year that passed by he had never missed a single day. His daily walk was one thing he was not willing to sacrifice. He was glad that even though his sleeping routine had changed completely his walking routine remained much the same with no changes in it at all.

Every morning after his duty was over and after his customary tea along with Ganesh, Aryan would go straight to bed without any breakfast for he was never hungry at that hour. He would sleep till three in the afternoon, soundly and peacefully always, and then after waking up he would start preparing a meager lunch. He never cared much for food. He just ate to satisfy his hunger and not for any taste or pleasure. He ate to survive.

He cooked simple dishes that could be prepared quickly and eaten quickly. He hated wasting time on eating. It seemed to him like it was a useless time-consuming activity that must be finished off as quickly as possible so that better things could be done.

And so he prepared rice every day, which he bought with his monthly salary, and any simple curry which could be prepared quickly.

He usually took ten to fifteen minutes to eat his lunch and that too only because Vincent had once told him that eating too fast was not healthy for the body. It was a bad habit, Vincent had told him. And since then he had made a deliberate effort to avoid eating too fast. Not because he had understood the logic behind it but out of respect for Vincent.

After his lunch he would have a cold bath and freshen up. And by four in the afternoon he would be all ready to leave for his walk. He would walk under the harsh sun, truly enjoying the heat and the tiredness. He enjoyed the experience of sweating and the heat surrounding and tiring him and his head slightly aching due to the punishment inflicted by the sun and his legs paining and slowing down. He enjoyed it all, and he would walk freely and randomly with a smile on his face, ignoring all the pain and discomfort. He loved walking at this hour under the relenting sun while everyone else sought to avoid it.

Why did he like walking in this heat so much? he wondered. Why did he like to sweat and get tired? Why did he like the feeling of his legs paining and getting heavy? Why did he like to torture his head under the harsh rays of the sun? he asked himself. Why did he like to walk nonetheless, struggling and suffering with all these discomforts but greatly enjoying them at the same time? Why? he wondered.

Maybe it was because he spent the rest of his day just sitting idle and almost motionless, doing nothing and feeling nothing in his body and because he had to just sit there on a chair surrounded by silence and darkness for twelve long hours with no movement or activity. The only activity taking place then was the constant activity in his mind. But his body remained still then, inactive and unproductive.

Maybe that was why he liked to feel the heat on his body while he walked, warming his body up, charging it. Maybe that was why he liked to feel his head throbbing and his legs tiring and aching and his body sweating. It made him feel alive. His body felt productive as if it were finally being used to its full capacity and for its actual purpose. Maybe that was why he craved so much for his afternoon walks, he thought, because the discomfort and suffering made him feel truly alive.

Or maybe he was just weird and different, he concluded. That was a possibility that could not be ignored, he thought, and then he laughed at his thinking again but he knew it had some truth to it.

He would walk on, looking around like a tourist, peeping into shops and window-shopping and looking at the buildings and the slums and the traffic and the never-ending crowd of people walking by. And he would take it all in, absorbing it and relishing it. But in the end, after he had walked and walked, he would always end up in a park to rest his tired body. That was always the final destination. No matter where he walked to or where he walked from he always ended up in some park. And he would sit there on a bench under the shade of a tree.

It was usually around five-thirty when he would reach there and settle down on a bench. And then for the next forty-five minutes he would dream. He would dream of his mother. Almost always of his mother. He missed her. He would daily wonder how she was getting along, how she was surviving. He would wonder if she was healthy and if she was enjoying life. He hoped that she was not miserable, that she was not suffering from poverty or loneliness or from some illness or disease.

Then he would force himself to stop thinking in such a negative way and make a conscious effort to get rid of all negative thoughts. He would always find it very difficult at first, almost impossible, for we human beings loved to think of misery and suffering and pain, whether it was ours or someone else's. It did not matter. It was irresistible. We enjoyed thinking of those terrible things more than we enjoyed thinking of good things. We get a kick out of it. But we never admit it. Instead we just lie to ourselves for lying was comforting and soothing, like some medicine. It was safe and it protected us from our own guilt.

No one would ever admit that they found pain

and suffering and misery much more fascinating than their opposites. No one would ever do that. Not even he himself, Aryan thought. He too would never admit to that even though it was true.

We only thought we liked listening to good news. We have convinced ourselves that we do. But that was false. We do not. For we always secretly anticipate hearing some bad news. It excited us and amused us, especially when it was related to someone else. Everyone loved tragedy. Everyone loved the drama that inevitably comes with bad news. And that fact could not and must not be denied, Aryan told himself, for no fact could ever be denied. It was impossible. It was best to just accept it and move on.

But there was good news, Aryan reminded himself while sitting on the bench and staring at nothing. The good news was that it was not our fault. Not at all. In fact it was no one's fault. No one was responsible for this crude and inhuman trait of ours for it was inherent in us. We could not help it. We were helpless. We were victims ourselves. It was already inbuilt within us, a part of us. It could not be separated from us. It was in our genetics, in our very soul, this perverse love for bad news and tragedy and pain and suffering and misery.

We did not choose it to be that way. We never had a choice. We did not acquire it as a habit. We all possess it because we were born with it. It was basic human nature. And so, because of that very reason, no one was really bad if they thought that way. No one could be blamed nor could anyone be judged on it. Thus, we were all absolved. The entire human race was absolved.

Then Aryan would stop thinking. He thought too much about everything, he would scold himself. He hated that habit of his. Then he would look at his surroundings for a few minutes and try hard to restrict his thoughts from flowing and overflowing. He would try to distract himself by looking at the children playing or the couples walking hand in hand or the senior citizens gossiping in a large group after their short evening walks.

And then a smile would come over his face. His heart would relax. He would feel calmer. Then he would think of his mother again. But only positive thoughts now, happy ones. He would imagine her laughing with her friends, gossiping and eating with them, still young and beautiful as he remembered her. He would imagine her happy and content and healthy and enjoying life, free from all illnesses and diseases, free from poverty and loneliness, free from pain and misery and suffering.

He would imagine her thinking of him and waiting for him to come back home someday. Then he would imagine her reaction, speechless but excited, when he would surprise her by suddenly showing up one day soon. And then he would feel much better and more optimistic about life.

He was desperate to see her again, to see the smile on her face and to embrace her. He would make that happen soon, he had decided on several occasions. He would make that happen as soon as possible.

He had started saving up some money since he received his very first salary. And now, twelve months later, he had managed to save enough to go to Kornur and come back by train. He would stay there with his mother for two whole weeks, he had decided. He would spend all the time with her and he would get reacquainted with his beautiful village and with everyone he knew.

He had dreamt of this many times before and he was determined to turn it into a reality now. At last he had enough money to do that. He never failed to get excited when he thought of it. Next month he would go back to Kornur to surprise his mother, he had decided. Next month was the month.

Aryan had already spoken to his boss about it the previous month and his boss had given him the permission to go. His boss was very happy with his work at the garden. He was impressed. The garden was completely free from all trouble and nuisance now and Aryan had a heroic role to play in it, his boss had told him. And since he was so happy, he immediately agreed to grant Aryan a two-week holiday to go back to his village. And, out of sheer happiness, his boss went one step further and offered him an increase in his monthly salary. His new salary once he would get back from Kornur would be ten thousand rupees.

Aryan had been surprised to hear that and he had thanked his boss profusely. The first thought that had come to his mind when he heard of his increment was that he could finally start painting again. The additional three thousand rupees every month would be used for buying his painting materials, he had decided. He would probably have to wait for a month after he got back from Kornur before he could start painting again, but that was fine. One month was nothing, he told himself.

He had become quite excited from then on. At last he could start painting again and that too with the help of his own money and on his own terms. This was what he had been hoping for all along. He could start again and keep going and keep trying again and again until he would succeed.

He had not told Vincent anything yet, but he hoped to tell him soon along with the news of him going back to Kornur for holidays. Vincent would be so happy to see him get back to painting again, he thought and smiled.

CHAPTER 16

Aryan woke up by five in the morning as he was used to doing. His body's alarm clock would not allow him to sleep past five.

The first thing he did on waking up was to prepare tea for Vincent and himself. He made it in Kornur style, a little different from the tea they made in Mumbai. It was stronger.

He did not really like the tea made in Mumbai for somehow it was very different from the tea he used to have in Kornur. The tea he drank in Mumbai had too much milk in it, he thought. And it lacked a certain spice. He tried to think which one it was and he finally figured it out. It lacked cloves. Maybe that was the problem. He liked his tea stronger and with cloves. And so he put less milk and then searched for cloves to put in the tea. After searching for a couple of minutes he found the cloves in a bottle in the corner of a shelf. Then he proceeded to prepare the tea, hoping that Vincent would like it too.

He sat at the dining table to drink his tea and thought about what he would paint that day. The house was all dark apart from a little light coming from a lamp near the dining table. He drank in solitude in the quiet darkness of the house. How should he start painting? he wondered. What would be his subject?

He had no subject. He tried very hard to remember the abstract paintings he saw in Rashid's gallery. Cubist and fauvist and surrealist and some other weird ones. He remembered them fairly well, not the names but the paintings.

It would be a difficult job to paint like that, he thought. It was easier to remember them than to emulate them. He had never painted like that before and he had a feeling that it would take him longer than expected to master such a style. He had to see and observe many such paintings to get an idea of it. And he had to practice and practice, he thought. Practice a lot.

The challenging aspect of the task ahead excited him. He drank his tea slowly and peacefully. He liked the taste of it as it reminded him of Kornur. He searched for the clock and saw the time. It was five-thirty already. He finished his tea and washed his cup. And then he headed back to his room to start painting.

He set up his canvas on the stand. Then he took out his paintbrushes and kept them on the bed. He chose one at random for he had no idea what he was going to paint or how he was going to do it. He was not used to so many options. Options had always confused him. He brought out the tubes of paints and the palette and he placed them on the small table next to the canvas. Then he filled a mug with water and kept it on the table too.

He was all ready to paint now. He looked at the time again. It was five forty-five. He had never painted like a professional before, so he was a little hesitant to begin. What if he messed up? he thought. But he had to start somewhere, he decided, and so he did.

He started randomly, keeping in mind what he had seen at the gallery, and he continued randomly. He painted for little more than an hour without realizing the time flying by. The sun had risen and its rays had entered his room without him knowing. He heard a knock on the door and then the door opened up slightly. Vincent's head peered in through the gap.

"Good Morning," Aryan said.

"Good Morning," said Vincent.

Vincent walked toward Aryan and stood facing the canvas. He looked at the work in progress.

"Not bad," Vincent said.

"Not good is more like it," Aryan said.

"Don't be so hard on yourself," Vincent said. "You have just started. Such things take a lot of time. And luckily time is all you have."

Vincent laughed at his own joke. Aryan tried to control his laughter at first but then he joined in too.

"That's true," said Aryan, laughing.

"Be patient with yourself, you are only human," Vincent said and walked out of the room.

Aryan checked the time again. It was seven. He took a break and went out into the living room. They both sat down at the dining table to have their breakfast. They had bread and an omelet each and Aryan was truly enjoying it as he had never eaten it before.

Vincent told Aryan that he loved the tea and then he asked what Aryan had put in it. Aryan said he had put in cloves and less milk. Vincent made a mental note of it.

They ate in silence for a few minutes. Then Vincent said, "What do you plan to do for the rest of the day?"

"Paint," said Aryan. "As much as possible."

"Don't forget to eat something. And roam about a little to get familiar with Mumbai."

"I was thinking of doing that," said Aryan. "I wanted to go to Rashid's gallery to see some paintings. I need more ideas."

"Yes, you must do that. But don't go too far also. If you get lost somewhere don't expect me to come searching for you," Vincent joked.

Aryan smiled at him. "I won't, don't worry," he said.

By nine Vincent left for work and Aryan was left behind to paint. He was alone now and the house fell silent. He would be alone till at least eight or nine at night until Vincent would get back home. He must get used to this solitude, he said to himself.

Vincent had given him a free reign. He had

shown Aryan how to start the TV and the air conditioner. But he did not need them now. He got back into his room and continued to paint till noon, struggling and hesitating all along, but continuing nonetheless. He had still not completed his painting for he lacked direction.

He took a break to have a meager lunch. He had painted enough for the morning, he thought, and so he decided to go to Rashid's gallery to have a look at those paintings again.

He went walking there, and he looked all around while walking like a tourist would do. There was noise and chaos all around and everywhere he looked it was crowded. He was amused by the sight of so many people constantly in motion.

The roads were packed with cars and bikes and rickshaws and buses and people. Once he also saw a horse-drawn carriage waiting at a signal just like all the other vehicles. The footpaths were surprisingly empty. He noticed that people preferred to walk on the roads along with the vehicles rather than walk on the footpaths. Kornur had no footpaths but he still knew that they were meant to be walked upon. It was such a peculiar habit, he thought. He wondered why they did that.

After walking on the footpath for ten minutes he came to understand why people preferred to walk on the road. He saw that the footpaths were almost completely occupied with little roadside food stalls and juice stalls and cigarette shops and fruit and vegetable stalls and paan shops and tea stalls and barber shops and cobblers and shoe polishing shops and trees and open gutters and all kinds of garbage and the occasional dog shit.

And after that ten-minute experience he too started walking on the road just like all the others. Clearly the footpath was not intended for walking purposes, he realized.

He walked slowly and leisurely, and after walking for twenty minutes he finally arrived at Rashid's gallery. Rashid was surprised to see him and he welcomed him with a big smile. Aryan told Rashid his purpose for visiting again and Rashid allowed him complete access to his gallery.

Aryan thanked him. Then he remembered and asked shyly, "Any update on my paintings?"

"Oh, not yet," said Rashid. "Don't worry. Such things take time."

Rashid smiled at him. Aryan smiled back gently, mostly because he remembered that Vincent had told him the same thing that morning.

Rashid took Aryan to where his paintings were displayed on the ground floor. Aryan was overwhelmed by the sight of his three paintings all properly framed now. He found it difficult to believe that they were his very own. He had painted them in the seclusion of his little house and now they were openly displayed on the walls of this huge posh gallery. He was speechless for a moment. It was a surreal experience for him. For the first time in his life he was truly proud of himself.

After he had satisfied himself by gazing at his own creations he turned toward the actual purpose of his visit. He went around looking at all the other kinds of paintings displayed on those walls. There were many to observe and learn from, and that was what he hoped to do.

He spent two hours observing each and every painting in the gallery. He searched for inspiration and he hoped he had found some. Once he was done he went to say goodbye to Rashid. He reminded Rashid, as a matter of formality, to inform him when his paintings were sold. Rashid said he would. Aryan was happy when he left the gallery and he walked back home. He could not wait to get back and start painting again.

He reached back home much quicker than he had reached the gallery. It was already five in the evening. He shut himself in his room and started painting again, keeping in mind all the different paintings he had seen.

He continued to paint till eight until his concentration was broken by the sound of the bell. It was Vincent. He was back from work. That was when Aryan realized that it was already eight and he decided to stop painting for the day even though he had still not completed his painting.

They ordered their dinner from a local restaurant and then they sat on the sofa and had it while watching a cricket match. They barely spoke to each other while they ate and watched. Aryan had never seen anything on TV before. He did not have one in Kornur and he had never felt the need for one. And so he watched the match with great fascination for the TV and the match were both a novelty for him.

"This is amazing," Aryan said with his eyes fixed on the screen.

"What is?" Vincent asked, chewing his food.

"This TV and this match both."

"Oh yes," said Vincent. "I can't live without TV now. I need to watch something while eating. Can't do without it."

"I don't blame you," said Aryan. "I always ate my food looking down at the plate. But this is definitely more interesting."

Vincent nodded and swallowed his food with difficulty and then said, "It is."

By eleven Aryan went to bed.

CHAPTER 17

One evening while Aryan was sitting on a bench in a park he saw an old man walking around, going from person to person with a half-cut plastic bottle in his hand and begging in the name of God.

The old beggar was wearing ragged worn-out clothes that were dirty and discolored. He had a wrinkled face and a long dirty-grey beard and he had a head full of shabby grey hair. He looked as if he had not washed himself for months. His grey hair was dirty and stiff and so was his grey beard. The old man was walking with naked feet on shaky legs and his back was severely bent and his hands were trembling.

Aryan stared at the old beggar with a keen eye. He watched the old man's every movement intently, looking at his feet and hands and at his manner of walking. The beggar went around to people, turn by turn, constantly shaking the half-cut plastic bottle with coins in it.

Aryan heard him beg. He heard the man beg many times and he heard it very carefully. And he noticed that each time the beggar reached a person he begged them for money in the name of God.

Always in the name of God.

Aryan had heard this many times before in many different places. He had heard many beggars plead for money in the name of God. They always took God's name without fail. But Aryan had never paid much attention to it until this very day. And suddenly all those times when he had heard them beg in such a way came rushing back to him. He began thinking.

Why did they always take the name of God? he wondered. Why did they not just ask for money plainly because they needed it? Why did they always have to get God in the middle? Did they really need to justify themselves by taking God's name? he thought. Were people so blind as to not see that a fellow human being was in need? Did people really need the sanction of God to help a fellow man in need? It was all so silly, he said to himself. He could not understand it.

Aryan looked at the beggar now who was moving slowly with pain and uneasiness. He saw the beggar being given some coins by some people, while some ignored him completely and some rudely shooed him away. Some gave him the coins with a serious face and some with an expression of contempt or hatred or repulsion. But none of them had given it to him with a smile on their face out of love or sympathy or even pity. They gave it to him because they wished to get rid of him as soon as possible.

But there was one thing in common between

the ones who gave him money, the ones who ignored him, and the ones who shooed him away. And that was the fact that they were all equally glad to get rid of him. They were all relieved to see him turn and walk away from them. Their faces relaxed and got back to normal. Some of them smiled out of relief and happiness. And Aryan sat there noticing everything like a judge who was about to condemn someone.

What we human beings had become, Aryan thought with frustration. We had become inhuman creatures, ungrateful and shameless. A fellow human being of ours was in dire need and we couldn't care less. And instead of helping him we found it easier to ridicule him in secret in our perverted minds. That was what the human race had come down to, he thought. We had fallen to a new low.

Aryan stopped thinking for a moment. He realized that he was judging every one of them and that too unjustly. He was also a part of that fallen human race, he reminded himself.

It was easy to judge from afar especially when others were involved, he realized. The faults of other people showed easily and bluntly, ready for judgment and ridicule. But it was almost impossible to judge ourselves, he thought. We found it difficult to see our own faults, thereby making us look perfect in our own image. And even if we succeeded at seeing our own faults clearly and bluntly it was still more difficult to actually judge and ridicule ourselves. And that was the most important part for then it becomes quite impossible to condemn ourselves.

Aryan stopped thinking again. He stared at the old beggar who was coming closer and closer to him now. He waited for him eagerly. He wanted the old man to come to him and ask him for money, and he wanted to give the old man a twenty-rupee note and not a one-rupee coin. And he wanted to do it with a smile on his face. He wanted to do it in the name of humanity and not in the name of God.

The old man finally came to him shaking the half-cut bottle with coins in it, the coins clinking against each other. Aryan looked up at the old man approaching him half bent. Aryan smiled gently. The old man stopped two feet ahead of Aryan and then stretched out his arm with the half-cut bottle. Then he shook the bottle and the coins clinked again. He looked at Aryan with sad tired eyes that were wrinkled and sagging.

Aryan looked back at him. His face was dark and Aryan caught a glimpse of his extremely thin wrist. The old man was severely malnourished. Aryan could not see the old man's mouth for it was covered under the thick dirty-grey beard.

Then the old man said in a soft trembling voice while jingling the coins simultaneously, "In the name of God please give some money. I beg you. God shall keep you happy if you do so. Please, in the name of God."

Aryan stared at the old man's face now, holding the twenty-rupee note in his right hand. The old man stared back at him. There was a brief moment of silence. And then Aryan suddenly remembered to smile and he did smile a big deliberate one. Then he stretched out his right hand with the twenty-rupee note in it and he put it in the half-cut bottle with respect and courtesy.

The old man looked at Aryan's smiling face and noticed the amount that Aryan had given him and he saw the manner in which Aryan had given it to him. The old man nodded slightly and then he smiled behind the dirty-grey beard.

Aryan noticed an upward twitch in the old man's beard that lasted for longer than a twitch normally does. He realized that the old man was smiling behind the beard and suddenly a great feeling of joy leapt within his heart and a broader smile appeared across his face. Aryan felt truly happy now.

The old man joined his hands in gratitude with the half-cut bottle between his palms and then he said in his weak voice, "Thank you, son. May God bless you."

"No, may you bless me, not God," Aryan said, still smiling.

The old man remained silent. His face was calm and relaxed. He stared at Aryan with his tired eyes but he said nothing.

"I give it to you in the name of humanity," Aryan said. "Not in the name of God."

The old man nodded again. He raised up his joined hands to Aryan and said, "Thank you very much. I wish more people were like you."

Aryan stared at him. The old man slowly turned to go away. He started walking.

"Why do you ask for money in the name of God?" Aryan asked the old man. "Why not in the name of humanity?"

The old man stopped walking. He stood there motionless. He waited. Then he slowly turned around again and faced Aryan and walked toward him and then stopped a few feet away from him. He smiled behind his dirty beard.

"You think I haven't tried that?" the old man said. "You think none of us have ever tried that?"

Aryan said nothing.

"We have all tried it and failed. We have tried it enough times to get discouraged and abandon it."

Aryan remained silent. He stared at the old man.

"In the name of humanity!" the old man scoffed. "That's funny. Human beings don't care for other human beings. They never have. They don't care if we are humans or some other disgusting creature. No one cares about all that. They treat us just like how they would treat a dirty street dog or a rat. Now what is the point of living when you are forsaken by your fellow men?"

The old man came closer to Aryan now. His eyes were no longer tired. They were alive and bright with rage and indignation. His voice was no longer weak.

Then he said, "Do you mind if I sit beside you for some time? My old legs are weak and they need rest."

"Please, sit," Aryan said and shifted to one side of the bench to make space for the old man.

The old man settled down with a sigh of relief. He held the half-cut bottle carefully in his hands as if it were something precious. For him it was precious. It was his only possession and his only property. It dictated his next meal and his next sip of water. It dictated his survival.

"Thank you, son," the old man said.

Aryan smiled at him. The old man smiled back.

"Do you know what always works?" the old man asked.

Aryan shook his head.

"God," said the old man. "The name of God always works for us. The name of God saves us from death. It keeps us on this beautiful planet among these terrible and greedy and self-centered creatures called human beings. Taking the name of God protects us for only then our generous fellow humans help us. Not otherwise."

"I understand," Aryan said.

"No you don't," said the old man. "You don't understand how cruel this world can be and how inhuman we humans can actually become. You don't understand how bad it can be."

"Why do people only help in the name of God?" Aryan asked. "Shouldn't our first responsibility be toward our fellow human beings?"

"It should be," said the old man leaning back on the bench. "But it's not. And the answer is quite simple actually. The reason people only help when God's name has been taken is because they fear God. They are afraid of their Gods. You think people do it because they love their Gods?"

"I don't know."

"They don't. They don't help us because they love their Gods. They only do it because they are scared of their Gods. They are afraid of the punishment that they believe their Gods will inflict upon them. That's all! Not for humanity's sake, not out of love or sympathy, not out of pity or kindness. That's all nonsense. Utter nonsense!"

The old man stopped talking to catch his breath. He breathed heavily now, wheezing and coughing. He had tired himself out. But he was not done yet and Aryan could sense that. The old man was only collecting his breath to continue again. Aryan waited in silence without uttering a word.

"All they want is to stay on the right side of God," the old man continued. "They want to be on the safe side, on the good side. People fear God thinking they are committing a sin by not helping us. And we take advantage of their fear. I admit it. And I don't regret it. Never. We have no choice but to take advantage of it. How else would we survive?"

Aryan nodded.

"So you see," the old man continued, "people

don't help us to protect us, they do it to protect themselves. To protect themselves from the wrath of God. And when you think about it it's all very funny."

The old man laughed. His entire body shook when he did so. Aryan looked at him and laughed too.

"It is funny," Aryan said.

"Do you know the only place where we don't have to take the name of any God for them to give us money?"

Aryan shook his head.

"In the house of God," the old man said and laughed again louder than before. "Didn't you ever wonder why so many beggars like me sit in front of places of worship? Because we don't need to take the name of God in such places as we are sitting in a place where God's influence still reigns supreme, near his very house. And so people give us wholeheartedly out of fear. They are afraid to ignore us so close to a place of worship. They feel that their God is watching them and judging them and condemning them and so they give and give with false smiles and false sympathy and false pity. It's all false charity. It's all an act displayed for their Gods."

Aryan became serious now. He no longer listened to the old man with amusement. He listened to him as a student would listen to a respected teacher. He listened with genuine interest, hanging on to every word of the old man, paying perfect attention. The old man was wise, he had wisdom, Aryan said to himself. It was evident. He waited for the old man to continue.

The old man looked at him and smiled. The sun had disappeared below the horizon but there was still enough light in the sky. The air was cooler now. It was already six-fifteen.

"But don't worry," the old man said, "the world is not as bad as it looks. It's not as unjust as it appears. It's a beautiful world."

"It doesn't look so beautiful," Aryan said.

"You must have faith," the old man said with a smile. "Sometimes it's very important to believe in something without any evidence or even in spite of evidence for it may give you hope. It may keep you alive and sane. Without it you can't achieve the impossible. We must have faith in mankind in spite of us constantly destroying each other. We must have faith that one day everything will be fine and that there will be peace everywhere and that humanity will become our common religion. We must necessarily have faith to achieve all those things."

Aryan stared at the old man.

"I think I have scared you," said the old man, laughing. "You have a lot of life to see yet. You must form your own conclusions. Life is beautiful."

The old man stopped talking. Aryan looked at the ground in silence. It was getting darker now, the light almost having left the sky. The sun was long gone. The park was getting empty.

The old man slowly stood up. Aryan stood up with him and looked up at the sky and realized that he was already late. Ganesh would be waiting for him.

"It's time for us to go, we are both late," the old man said, his voice weak again.

"It was nice talking to you," said Aryan.

The old man laughed. He started walking away. Then he said, "I'm just an old ignorant beggar. People call me crazy. But you are a good boy. You are human."

Aryan did not respond. He was left speechless by the wise old man. He watched the old man walk away, bent over, weak and struggling. That man was no ordinary man. That man was a sage, he thought, and then he turned and ran in the direction of the abandoned garden.

CHAPTER 18

Aryan followed the same routine for a week and he found that he was comfortable with it. It suited him to wake up early and to sleep early. He could be more productive that way, he felt. And so he kept up the same routine week after week without much variation in it.

He would get up at five in the morning every day and make tea for Vincent and himself. He would then sit at the dining table and drink the tea slowly and peacefully. By five forty-five he would start painting and he would paint continuously till seven when Vincent got up. Then they would have breakfast together. By nine Vincent would leave for work and Aryan would get back to his room to paint.

He would paint till noon and then he would eat his lunch and go for a walk in the afternoon or he would watch some random cricket match on TV. At five in the evening he would go back into his room and paint until eight or nine at night when Vincent got back home. The two of them would then have dinner together in front of the TV. By eleven Aryan would go to bed and Vincent would either continue watching TV or get back to some work of his.

Aryan had taken more than a week to finish his first painting and the result had not satisfied him at all. Vincent was encouraging as usual but Aryan knew better. He was disappointed with his first work.

He had failed to realize how hard it was going to be. He had to work harder, he thought, and so he decided to keep a target for himself. He must not take more than a week to finish one painting, he decided. He did not have so much time in his hands.

He was very well aware of the fact that every day that he lived and painted in Vincent's house it was costing Vincent a good amount of money. His very existence in Mumbai was quite expensive for Vincent. He knew Vincent would not tell him anything but he could not take his generosity for granted. He refused to take such undue advantage of a man like Vincent.

On weekdays in the afternoons Aryan walked about the city, not too far from the places he knew but far enough to experience a new place every time. He visited gardens and parks almost every day and he sat there under the shade of the trees daydreaming about better days ahead. He hoped and dreamed there for hope was the only thing he possessed and dream was the only thing he could do.

He observed the endless stream of people walk

by on the roads and he marveled at their urgency to get somewhere, anywhere. He wondered why they were all so busy. What were they doing in life that was so important? Why were they always in such a hurry?

He could not understand. No one walked slowly. No one observed anything around them. No one had a smile on their face. They all looked down and walked as if they were terribly ashamed of something they had done. They did not look happy at all. Not in the least. They even ate in a hurry as if they were committing a grave sin. As if eating was a forbidden act. They gulped down their food, barely chewing it, and then they rushed back into the tall glass buildings where they worked.

The only act they did with leisure was smoking. Groups of working men and women would come out regularly at specific intervals and they would smoke their lungs away slowly and steadily. And then they felt at peace. Their faces would relax and a smile would appear on their faces for a few minutes and just as quickly their smiles would disappear and then they themselves would disappear again into the buildings.

Was this the life one got to live in this great city? Aryan wondered. Was this the reason why Mumbai seemed so attractive? Was this life really worth it? he asked himself. All he could see was sad and depressed people. People who worked all day and enjoyed nothing and who looked down and walked but never bothered to enjoy the view around them and who were in such a hurry that they never noticed their life passing by them and who lived so fast that they had forgotten how to slow down. They were all troubled souls.

If this was the life in Mumbai then he did not want it at all. He wanted no part of it. He preferred the life that Kornur offered its people for money could never afford happiness and happiness could never be ignored by being busy.

On weekends Aryan visited Rashid's gallery in the afternoons. He spent hours there observing and learning. He absorbed all he could and all he was capable of absorbing. He looked for inspiration but rarely found any. He asked Rashid on every weekend visit if any of his paintings had been sold and every time he got back the same reply, "No. Not yet."

Rashid would ask him how his paintings were coming along. Did he learn the new styles? Was he picking them up with ease? When was he going to submit a new one to the gallery? Aryan would reply to each question truthfully and honestly. He told Rashid about his struggle and about his inability to paint anything worthwhile. He was still struggling, he said. But he would get it soon, he always promised at the end.

On one such visit to the gallery Aryan noticed that only two of his paintings were on display now. The third one was missing. He went all around the gallery looking for the third painting but he could not find it. He finally asked Rashid about it and Rashid gave him the truth.

"Your paintings are not selling, Aryan," Rashid explained. "They are taking up space on those walls. Space which many other artists deserve too. We have to display the paintings of our other clients also, you see."

Aryan did not say anything. He understood the situation. Rashid was right in his own way. His paintings were ruining the chances of other paintings that could sell.

Then he asked in a sad tone, "And what about the other two?"

Aryan knew what the answer would be but he wished to hear it nonetheless.

"Well," Rashid said softly. He hesitated to speak. Then he said, "If they don't sell soon we may have to remove them too."

Aryan nodded faintly but did not speak.

"It's nothing personal, Aryan," Rashid said. "I will continue to support you. It's just, you know."

"Yes, I do," Aryan said with a forced smile.

"I have to look out for the others too. And my business."

"I understand," Aryan said.

He did not blame Rashid for anything. He just hoped that at least one of his paintings would sell before they were taken down.

On another visit Aryan noticed that another painting of his had been taken down. Only one was left up on the walls now. He did not question

Rashid about it and neither did Rashid offer any justification. It was understood.

He continued to look around at the paintings by different artists and he tried to improve on his paintings by keeping them in mind. He still struggled for these styles did not come as naturally to him as he had expected. He put in the hours but not the emotions.

Aryan kept to his one-painting-a-week rule and he even succeeded at it, but the results were not satisfactory. His paintings looked like amateur copies of other works. They lacked something vital that could only be fulfilled by his own creativity and not by merely copying other works. His paintings lacked his own magic touch and ingenuity and his emotions. They were all dead, not alive.

Nevertheless he kept at it day after day and week after week and month after month. He had not lost all hope yet. His vigorous painting routine continued as it slowly became his only safe haven where he could lose himself completely in his art without worrying about anything else.

Finally, on another weekend visit to the gallery, Aryan saw what he was afraid to see. He saw that his only painting that was left up on the walls had also been taken down once and for all. Not a single one could be sold.

He remembered what Rashid had told him at their first meeting. Rashid was right, Aryan said to himself. No one cared for realistic paintings anymore. Those days were gone. And they were gone long ago. He was just not aware of it.

Rashid met Aryan on that day with a guilty expression on his face. He looked at Aryan but he did not say anything. Aryan looked back at him and smiled a small smile.

"I'm sorry," said Rashid. "I had to."

"You were right," Aryan said.

Rashid looked at Aryan and then he looked down. He did not respond to that.

"Would you like to see the new ones?" Rashid said, changing the topic.

"I would love to," Aryan said.

Rashid took him around the gallery and showed him the different styles of different artists. Aryan looked and listened to Rashid with a sense of detachment. He feigned interest while Rashid showed him around and he observed with not the same keen eye as before. Rashid stressed on the importance of uniqueness in an artist's work.

"The paintings of an artist must reveal the individuality of the artist," Rashid said.

Aryan nodded.

"They must reveal the personality of the artist," Rashid said.

Aryan nodded in understanding again.

"Every artist must discover his own voice and express it through his art," Rashid said and Aryan nodded.

"The artworks of an artist must be unique when compared to all the other artists. Only then can an artist stand out from the rest," Rashid said.

Aryan nodded again, slowly and deliberately. He had listened to Rashid's wisdom but he had not registered it completely. He had nodded at the right time and in the right way. Rashid was happy thinking that Aryan had learned something from his discourse. He felt less guilty now.

But for Aryan it was very different. Everything that Rashid had said an artist must be he was exactly the opposite of that right now, he thought. His paintings did not reveal his personality. They did not possess his voice in them and they did not express anything. Nothing at all. They were devoid of any substance. They said nothing and showed nothing and meant nothing. They were merely poor caricatures of better works by better artists and were not at all unique in any way. They were dead creatures with no life and no soul. They existed just for the sake of it and not for any purpose. There was no way they could stand out from the rest.

That evening he reached home and he did not paint. He sat down on the bed and thought about what Rashid had said. He wondered why his paintings lacked all those qualities.

And then he found the answer. He himself was the answer to all those problems. He did not have a voice of his own. He had not discovered it yet. Was he unique in any way? He doubted it. Did he possess a good enough personality? He was not so sure. And did he really stand out from the rest? No.

He did not. He was just like everyone else. He was a sheep in a flock and not a lion in the wild.

He was not surprised anymore. How could he expect his paintings to possess the very qualities that he lacked himself? He could not. Sitting there on the bed he realized that he could never succeed unless he fixed himself. His paintings were his own reflection. They would only stand out from the rest when he stood out from the rest.

CHAPTER 19

"When did you decide all of this?" Vincent asked Aryan.

"A couple of weeks ago," Aryan said, chewing his lunch.

"And when are you going?"

"At the end of this month."

"For how long?"

"Two weeks."

"I see," Vincent said and paused to swallow the food. Then he drank some water. "And what about your train ticket?"

"I have already purchased it," Aryan said, his eyes fixed on the TV. A cricket match was on.

"When did you do that?" asked Vincent, surprised.

"A week ago or something. Why?"

"And I didn't even know about all this," Vincent said and shook his head.

"I wanted to surprise you," Aryan said and looked at Vincent with a big smile, his mouth full with food.

"Well it wasn't a good surprise then."

"Oh come on."

"But I'm happy," Vincent said proudly. "It's time you visit your mother. She must be anxious to hear from you and to see you."

"I'm anxious to see her too," Aryan said.

"I hope she's fine. I hope she got along well without you."

"I hope so too. I can't wait to get back. I can't wait to see her."

"I will come to drop you at the station."

"You don't have to trouble yourself," Aryan said politely.

"Keep quiet," Vincent said, looking at the TV.

Aryan laughed. Then they ate in silence for a few minutes. It was a pleasant Sunday afternoon. It was Aryan's cricket-watching day.

"I thought you would be more excited to hear that I'm getting back to painting," said Aryan.

"I am," Vincent said. "That's great news. I was afraid you had given up altogether."

"I almost had to be very honest," Aryan said. "But your speech saved me. I thank you for that."

"My speech? What speech?"

"You knocked some sense into me that day," Aryan said, smiling. "You were right, I was making excuses."

"Yes you were. I told you that."

"You did. And you were absolutely right. I thought a lot about what you told me that day."

"You did?"

"Yes. My job allows me a lot of time to do that," Aryan said and laughed. Vincent smiled at him.

"That's true," said Vincent.

"I admit I was wrong."

"Yes you were."

"But there's some truth to it, and I still believe that," said Aryan. "But you were right. We can't achieve anything in life by just submitting to fate or by relying on the natural course our life takes."

"That's right," said Vincent. "We must go out there and try to change our fate. And we can do it."

"I agree," Aryan said and nodded.

"I'm glad you came back to your senses. Now you can do what you were born to do."

Aryan smiled but he did not say anything. He had a vague feeling of optimism, a feeling that everything would turn out fine.

"Do you have enough money yet to start painting?" Vincent asked.

"No," Aryan replied. "But once I get my salary after coming back from Kornur I can start.

"In case you need any help," Vincent said and trailed off, knowing quite well that it was a sensitive subject.

Aryan looked at Vincent and chuckled. Then he said, "I don't. I have waited for so long already, some more time waiting won't hurt me."

"That's true," Vincent said. "Your job has taught you to be patient."

"It really has," said Aryan. "Patience is all that keeps me sane there."

They switched channels for some time. They put on an old Hindi movie and watched it until they were bored after ten minutes. Then they watched the news for a couple of minutes but there was nothing interesting going on other than the usual political propagandas. They went back to watching cricket.

They did not talk to each other for a long time, both completely lost in the match and too tired to make conversation.

Then finally Aryan said, "Any news from Rashid about the paintings?"

"Nothing yet," Vincent replied as usual.

Then they continued to watch the match in silence.

CHAPTER 20

Six months had passed by and Aryan had achieved nothing. The little hope that he had possessed had abandoned him by now.

Those three paintings of his had been his only hope during his struggle to create something new. The knowledge of them being displayed and possibly being sold had kept his spirits high. And so until the last one had not been taken down he still had some hope. But that hope was taken away from him when Rashid had brought down his last painting. That last one had come to symbolize his last hope, and when that was brought down his last hope had come crumbling down too.

Aryan was also conscious of being a burden on Vincent now and his gratitude had slowly turned into guilt. Vincent continued to encourage him by telling him not to lose hope and not to give up and not to surrender to despair. But for Aryan it was easier said than done. It was difficult to have hope when he had nothing going on for him. It was easy to give up. It was comforting to surrender.

During one of their conversations Aryan confessed his feeling of guilt for being a burden on

Vincent. He was a bad investment, he told Vincent. But Vincent disagreed. He told Aryan that he was free to live in his apartment for as long as he desired and that he was not an investment. He was no burden, Vincent told him, and he should not feel guilty about it.

There was silence for a few minutes. Neither of them spoke. Vincent looked at Aryan but Aryan refused to look back at him. He kept his eyes on the floor. His palms were sweaty.

"Is any son just an investment to his father?" Vincent asked. "Is any child just an investment to the parents?"

Aryan did not say anything.

"And besides, I like living with you. I have some company now. You are like the son I never had."

Aryan smiled. He felt a little better now although he was not fully convinced.

Then he suddenly asked Vincent, "But why did you never marry?"

"That's a long story," Vincent said. "And a boring one. I will tell it to you some other day."

Aryan laughed.

For a couple of months after their conversation Aryan felt a renewed passion for painting. A flicker of hope returned again. He followed the same routine and he even succeeded in making some progress.

His paintings were coming along fairly decently although not as good as he would have liked. But there was an improvement in his paintings that was clearly noticeable. He found it easier as compared to before but he still stuck to his one-painting-a-week rule. He perfected each one until he was properly satisfied with the result and then he moved on to the next one.

But he never considered submitting those paintings to the gallery for he waited to create better ones. The paintings he had been creating now were good but they were not good enough to be displayed on those walls. And he was aware of that. Only once he had mastered his style would he dare to submit them. He knew he would achieve that someday but he did not know how long it would take.

In the meantime he also tried to work on his Hindi. He wanted to perfect the language. It was too broken now and it desperately needed some serious mending. He found it very difficult to speak to people and understand them properly. Many times he had to ask them to repeat what they said and many times they had to ask him to repeat what he said. And every time this misunderstanding led to some confusion. Sometimes minor and more often than not major.

He spoke the language cautiously and slowly and he took time to process it and understand it. Due to this disability he purchased wrong tickets on the bus and he got down at the wrong stops. Rickshaw drivers dropped him at the wrong places because he told them the wrong places. Shopkeepers gave him the wrong products and he accepted them all without complaining for he was afraid to argue with them in a language he was not at all fluent in. He always figured that it must have been his mistake.

And as if the problem of not knowing Hindi properly was not enough he quickly found out that many people in Mumbai also spoke another language which he had never heard before. That language was Marathi. It seemed quite similar to Hindi in script but not so much in speech.

Marathi confused him to no end. At least he had heard and picked up a little bit of Hindi in Kornur as most people in Kornur spoke broken and inconsistent Hindi just like him. But he had never heard anyone speak Marathi in Kornur. He found out much later that it was a regional language that was spoken mainly in and around the state of Maharashtra.

Aryan decided to concentrate and improve on his Hindi for now. Vincent offered to help him. The two of them came to an understanding that they would only speak in Hindi at home. They decided to watch Hindi movies and Hindi news channels and see cricket matches only with Hindi commentary. They also decided to hear Hindi songs every morning without fail.

For some reason Vincent seemed much more excited about the whole project. Aryan just went with the flow.

CHAPTER 21

The days passed by quickly without Aryan even realizing it. It was nearing the end of the month now and in two days he would be leaving for Kornur. His ticket was ready and he had already begun packing his stuff for the two-week trip.

He was very excited. Every time he thought about going back a big smile would involuntarily appear on his face and his heart would beat with excitement. Every day since he had purchased the train ticket he dreamt of going back. He dreamt of how he would spend his two weeks over there. And he did that the entire day, while on duty and while sleeping and while walking and eating.

He had decided that one day before leaving for Kornur he would take a holiday and go to collect his salary so that he would have enough money for his stay in Kornur. He also wished to buy a few things in order to give them as gifts there. He wanted to buy something for his mother and for his neighbors, especially Raja's family, for they had helped him a lot when he was in need.

But he was still confused as to what he should buy. Whatever he decided to buy had to be within his meager budget. He did not have the luxury to buy according to his likes and dislikes. He had to be very careful in spending his money, Vincent had taught him. And he had learned it well. He was sufficiently good at managing his finances now.

Aryan thought about the gifts a lot, more than was really necessary. He spent hours on end trying to figure out who would like what and in the end he always dismissed whatever he had decided. He consulted three people regarding the gifts and he got three very different answers in return which left him even more confused than before.

First he asked Vincent and Vincent advised him that he should give a beautiful sari to his mother, and he liked that idea. A sari seemed to be an appropriate gift for his mother. It would be perfect for her. She would love it. And for his neighbors Vincent had suggested multiple things, none of which had satisfied him.

And so Aryan asked Ganesh. Ganesh advised him to buy statues or posters of Gods and Goddesses. Aryan thought he was joking but Ganesh made it very clear he was not. Aryan did not like his suggestion. But Ganesh insisted on it, saying it was the best gift to give anyone. Aryan regretted asking Ganesh for advice.

Then at last Aryan asked Bittu for his opinion. Bittu was quite flattered that Aryan had cared to ask him and he quickly suggested that Aryan should give them posters of either cricketers or movie stars and nothing else. Aryan shook his head in regret. Bittu was convinced that everyone liked cricketers and movie stars. Aryan disagreed with him. But Bittu insisted on it, saying he would have loved it if someone had gifted him that. Aryan ignored Bittu's suggestion.

A few days later, on Vincent's suggestion, Aryan finally decided to buy sweets for his neighbors. Sweets were the safest and most conventional gift to give anyone since time immemorial. No one would ever object to being gifted sweets, he thought.

On the evening before Aryan was supposed to leave Vincent took him around the city in his car to buy whatever he had decided to buy. Aryan had collected his salary that morning itself and his boss had very kindly wished him a safe journey. He was ready to spend now.

First they went to a sari shop to buy one for his mother. Aryan had no idea what was considered a good sari and so he asked Vincent to help him out. Vincent refused to do so for he too had no idea how to buy saris. Did he look like someone who knew how to buy saris? Vincent asked Aryan. Aryan agreed he did not.

Because of their inability to choose a good sari they decided to make the shopkeeper responsible for providing them with a good one. They told him that they trusted him completely and that they had complete faith in him and that they depended on him. The shopkeeper nodded a few times in agreement and promised to give them a sari of the best quality at the most reasonable rate.

The shopkeeper went on to suggest various saris to choose from, mentioning their material and rates and the discounts he could give on them. He also gave his expert opinion on which one should be bought according to him. Aryan and Vincent nodded mechanically at whatever he said, not understanding a word but pretending to understand everything.

Aryan suddenly remembered his mother's favorite color which she had mentioned to him once in his childhood. He was surprised to remember it all of a sudden as he had not even attempted to think of it. That vague and distant memory had come out of nowhere and it had made itself very clear in his mind. He smiled in wonder.

His mother's favorite color was blue. Blue like the sea, she had told him. He remembered it very well. And now he knew which sari he had to select. The choice was simple and obvious now.

"Give me that blue one," Aryan told the shopkeeper.

The shopkeeper nodded and said that it was the best and most reasonably priced one with the most perfect material.

But Aryan did not care about all that. He was thinking of something else with a gentle smile on his face. He was thinking of his mother again. He was not buying the blue sari for its perfect material or for its reasonable price. He was buying it simply because it was blue like the sea.

The shopkeeper quickly packed the sari and then mentioned again the discount he could give on it. Aryan accepted it without bothering to bargain any further. Any price was worth that color for him now.

It turned out to be a little more expensive than what he had expected to spend but he happily paid for it without any regret. Vincent offered to buy it for him but he refused any help. He had to buy it with his own money, he told Vincent, for only then would it be significant and only then could he be proud of himself.

Vincent relented but he also insisted on buying another one as his gift to Aryan's mother. Aryan told him he did not have to do that. Vincent said he wanted to gift her something to pay his respects and give his regards. Aryan relented.

Vincent selected a green sari for Aryan's mother. The shopkeeper readily gave his approval, stating that it was also one of the best and most reasonably priced ones with the most perfect material. Aryan and Vincent both chuckled on hearing the same line again.

"I think she will like this," said Vincent. "It's green like the trees."

"I hope not more than the one I selected," said Aryan.

"You are just jealous. You are feeling threatened by my choice."

Aryan laughed and said, "I am, I won't deny it."

The shopkeeper quickly packed the sari and

offered his discount. Vincent quickly paid for it and then they left the shop.

Vincent took Aryan to a famous sweets shop. Aryan did not know anything much about Mumbai sweets and here Vincent took charge of the situation. Vincent was an expert at purchasing sweets and he selected the most eclectic ones, all different looking and different tasting, and Aryan only stood there observing him.

After the sweets had been selected Aryan asked for five boxes to be packed with those sweets. Within ten minutes of entering the shop they were already out of it and inside the car. Then they went to a seafood restaurant to have their dinner.

By ten they were done with their dinner and they went back to Vincent's house. It was almost eleven by the time they reached there. They were both very tired. It had been a long and tiring day for them. Before going to bed Vincent asked Aryan what time his train was the following day. Aryan told him it was at nine at night. Then Vincent went to bed and Aryan went into his room.

Aryan looked at his old paintings that were wrapped up carefully in bubble wrap. Nostalgia struck him again. He did not unwrap them but he just stared at them through the bubble wraps and recollected all those days he had spent in this room painting and painting and painting. And those paintings were the results of his hard work, all of them hiding behind bubble wraps now, too ashamed to come out and show themselves.

He was ashamed to bring them out too. Those were not even the best ones he had created, he thought, sinking deeper into the painful trap of nostalgia. The best ones could not even be sold, he reminded himself. That was so sad. That was pitiful, he thought. All that hard work had got him to what? he wondered.

And then he restrained his thoughts. His thoughts were drifting away in the wrong direction again and he quickly realized it. And so he stopped them and then got rid of them.

There could be no room for negativity now. This was all the doings of nostalgia, he told himself. Evil nostalgia that made us think of negative stuff and then gave us pleasure out of it. It made us think of sad and depressing stuff and allowed us to derive pleasure from it and allowed us to enjoy it and then got us addicted to it. And then, all of a sudden, the pleasure we derived from it disappears in an instant and the only thing that was left behind was the negative stuff, the sad and depressing stuff and the pain that it caused.

So he forced his mind to go blank. He laid down on the bed and closed his eyes and then he forced himself to think about the day when he would start painting again. That day was not too far away, he reminded himself. That day was quite close. He could almost touch it. Maybe a little more than a month away, he thought. Or at the most two months away. And then he could start again.

He imagined himself painting daily before

work in his little shed in the abandoned garden. He would be completely free to create and make mistakes and he would be free from all distractions and be free to paint whatever he wanted to paint.

He started to smile and his smile widened across his face. The trap of nostalgia had been overcome. He felt relaxed now. His optimism, which always abandoned him when nostalgia struck him, had returned. And it had returned stronger than ever before as it always did without fail.

Around five in the morning he fell asleep.

CHAPTER 22

Nine months had passed since Aryan had come to Mumbai.

He had practiced for too long now and he was ready to churn out paintings that he could submit to Rashid. He took a whole month to create two paintings which he thought were good enough to be displayed in the gallery. They were both cubist portraits, one of a fisherman and the other of a fisherwoman.

He painted them because they were the only subjects he was comfortable with. That fisherman and fisherwoman represented Kornur better than anything else for him. They were the people of Kornur. They were the heart of it.

He was satisfied with what he had created although he could easily spot many flaws in them. There was still a lot of room for improvement, he thought. He had still not mastered the style yet. Vincent was impressed by Aryan's progress and he congratulated him on his achievement. But Aryan refused to take his compliments seriously.

"You are a bad judge I think," said Aryan.

"I don't think so," Vincent said coyly. "I like

these two paintings. They are really good."

"But those paintings at the start were terrible and you still complimented them."

"Let's just agree to disagree," Vincent smiled and said quickly, and then he walked away.

Aryan laughed. He knew Vincent had said all that just to encourage him. Without those early compliments he would never have been able to reach this far. He was truly grateful for those false compliments.

Aryan submitted those two paintings to Rashid one day and Rashid accepted them gladly. Then he led Aryan into his office so that they could talk in private and cut a new deal.

"How are they?" Aryan asked Rashid.

"They are good. I'm impressed," Rashid said.

"Will they sell?"

"Only time will tell, not me," Rashid said. "But they should. They are good. Just pray to God and everything will be fine."

Aryan smiled. Then he said, "For how long will you keep them up there?"

"A few months," Rashid replied. "Maybe three."

"Alright," Aryan said. He was happy with that.

Then they moved on to the uncomfortable part. They had to discuss and agree upon the price to be set for each painting and the splitting of the sale proceeds. This time Aryan did not have Vincent to negotiate for him. He felt confident enough to do it himself as he was now aware of how it all worked. He knew now how the art industry functioned. Experience had taught him enough.

After much informal discussion the two of them agreed to set the price at fifty thousand rupees for each painting. That was how much it would be worth in the local art market, Rashid said to Aryan. Aryan agreed with him.

In these nine months due to his many visits to the gallery he had learned to ascertain the value of paintings based on the local art market. The value of each painting depended upon the local market, and so a painting that was worth less in Mumbai could be worth a lot more in Delhi. He was aware of that fact. That was how the business worked.

And most importantly he had no great pretensions about his paintings. He knew they were not the best ones of their type and that they had many defects. In fact as he looked around at the paintings in the gallery he had to admit to himself that his paintings looked the least impressive when compared to the others.

So they agreed on the pricing and then they agreed on the percentage split of the sale proceeds. Just like the previous time they agreed that sixty percent of the proceeds would go to Aryan and the remaining forty percent would go to the gallery.

Aryan had found out that most galleries asked for the same percentage split and in fact some asked for even higher cuts. So he had no issues regarding the split for he thought it was a reasonable and beneficial one. All in all he was content. He signed the contract and they were both satisfied with it. He was a little proud of himself although he found it a bit silly to be proud of such a thing.

CHAPTER 23

Aryan woke up by noon and found that Vincent was not at home. He had gone to work.

Aryan stumbled into the kitchen to make tea for himself and he did so still half-asleep. His head felt heavy and his eyes were only half-open but he did not want to go back to sleep.

He spent the rest of the day packing whatever he thought was necessary. He carefully packed the saris and the sweets, making sure that no damage would be done to them during the journey. He repacked the few clothes that he had already packed, arranging and rearranging them again and again until he was satisfied.

After he was all done with his packing he felt at ease. Now he could just sit back and relax, he thought. All he had to do now was wait for Vincent to get back home in the evening.

He watched the repeat of an old cricket match in the afternoon with his eyes fixed on the screen but his thoughts somewhere in Kornur. His thoughts wandered about on the narrow streets of his village and on its beaches and over the blue sea with hundreds of little fishing boats floating on its surface, some parked near the shore, some out in the open waters.

His thoughts wandered through the crowded market which was vibrant and chaotic as ever with the smell of fish perpetually in the air. The smell of fish was the smell of his village, he thought and smiled. They could not be separated. It was impossible.

His thoughts traveled the outskirts of his village, the countryside full of tall coconut trees dancing to the rhythm of the sea breeze. He took great joy in thinking about that now. His heart began to beat with excitement again.

Around two-thirty in the afternoon he fell asleep on the sofa with the cricket match still on. He got up by five and he noticed that another repeat of an old cricket match was on. He was sweating from his forehead and he wiped off the sweat with his right palm.

He was feeling hungry now. He felt a little guilty about leaving the TV on all this while and so he switched it off immediately and remained sitting there on the sofa in a lethargic state. He rubbed his eyes with his fingers and then he rested his face on his palms. He was feeling quite lazy because of both sleep and lack of sleep. He wished Vincent would come home soon.

Then he suddenly decided to have a cold bath to shake off his lethargy and laziness. It always worked, he said to himself. After the cold bath he felt much better. He was refreshed and his mind was alert again and his eyes completely open. He felt energetic now.

In the kitchen he found a half packet of bread and he decided to eat it with butter and tea. He loved that combination. He loved it because it was quick and easy and tasty. After he was done eating his stomach calmed down again. The rumbling inside had come to an end. He was satisfied.

By six Vincent came back from work. Aryan was glad. Finally he had some company now. They decided to leave for the station by seven-thirty at least so they could reach on time even if there was terrible traffic, which was almost a certainty.

Vincent asked Aryan where he planned to have dinner and Aryan said he would buy something on the train itself and have it. Vincent asked him to be ready by seven-fifteen at least.

At seven-thirty they left for the station in Vincent's car. As they had expected, the traffic was terrible as usual but they managed to reach well on time. They had to wait for forty-five minutes for the train to arrive. The train was not too late. It arrived by nine-five, which was truly a great achievement.

It was finally time for Aryan to leave now. He thanked Vincent for driving him to the station. Vincent told him to shut up. They both looked at each other and laughed and then they embraced each other warmly.

"Give my regards to your mother," Vincent told Aryan.

Aryan nodded.

"And do tell her that the green sari is from me and not you. Don't claim it for yourself."

"I won't," Aryan said and laughed. "Unless she hates the blue one. Then I will claim the green one without any guilt."

"In that case I will allow it," Vincent said with a smile.

They separated from each other. Aryan picked up his suitcase and looked at Vincent.

"See you soon," Vincent said.

"See you soon," said Aryan, and then he turned away and climbed into the train.

At the door Aryan turned around and looked at Vincent again. Vincent was smiling at him from the platform. Aryan stood at the door and smiled back, waving at Vincent for one last time. And then he disappeared inside.

At nine-ten the train departed.

CHAPTER 24

Aryan's command over the Hindi language was improving much faster than he had expected. He did not find it as difficult as he had thought it would be. He was getting fluent at speaking it and he now found it much easier to understand it too. It had barely been a couple of months since he had resolved to improve on his Hindi and he was already getting quite good at it.

As always Vincent was impressed. Vincent told Aryan that he had a knack for the language. Aryan disagreed. He believed that his broken Hindi had made it easier for him to grasp the language, which was true. The Hindi-talking rule at home and Hindi movies and Hindi news and Hindi songs and Hindi cricket commentary had all helped him to pick up the language quickly and well.

Aryan suddenly found himself with the ability to communicate with people without any difficulty. His life had become much easier and it was all because of Vincent, he thought. Vincent did not mind taking the credit for this for he had been very emotionally invested in this project for some reason.

After Aryan had submitted the two paintings to Rashid he had decided to take a break from painting. He had painted too much in the past nine months and he was a little tired and fed up now. He needed a break, a hiatus, and he needed it as soon as possible.

For the past nine months he had painted almost every single day. And it had already been quite expensive for Vincent, he thought, even though Vincent would never admit to that. Each day of those nine months had cost Vincent a good deal and he found it impossible to ignore that. It was something that had weighed heavily on his conscience even after they had spoken about it.

Vincent was too good to say anything, Aryan thought. If it was up to him he would even adopt Aryan. But for Aryan the guilt of living for free and depending on someone's charity was all too much to bear. At least in Kornur he had been independent, he thought. And now he longed to be independent again to earn his own money and livelihood so that he would not be an unnecessary burden on Vincent.

For how long could he stay in this way for free, without any responsibility or accountability? How long could he stay without contributing in any way other than preparing tea every morning? At least if he were contributing in any substantial way like paying rent for his stay or paying for the food or something or anything he would still feel a lot better.

But he was not. He had no money of his own. He ate Vincent's food for free. He stayed at Vincent's house for free. His painting materials were bought and given to him for free. Even the clothes he wore were bought and given to him for free. He realized that his whole life in Mumbai was sponsored by a kind soul and that he existed there only because of Vincent's charity and not because he had the ability or industry to do so. He was just a parasite, he thought.

He had decided after much careful thought that it was time for him to move out of Vincent's house. It would be better for him as well as for Vincent. He could not be a burden on Vincent anymore. He had to be independent. He needed the struggle. He had to learn to survive on his own. For how long could he live a sheltered life like this? he wondered. He was a man now and like a man he must behave, he thought. It was time to face the city on his own.

He had made this decision within a few days of submitting the paintings to Rashid. He decided to get a job somewhere, anywhere, so he could survive on his own until his paintings were sold. And he would try to get accommodation somewhere cheap. Somewhere where the rent could be covered with the money he earned. He was willing to live absolutely anywhere as long as he did it on his own.

But there were a few major hurdles in the execution of his plan. First, the obvious fact that it was going to be very difficult. He had many questions that he had no answers to. From where would he get a job? Who would give him a job when he possessed no valuable skill at all? He only knew how to draw and paint and the only trade he had some experience in was the fishing trade. And he hated that trade. He did not wish to become a fisherman again. Not in this life.

Second, he could not get a place to stay unless he got a job first. He had no money with him and so he could only move out once he was absolutely sure that he had a job.

And third, which was the most difficult problem to solve, the biggest hurdle, the problem of Vincent. How would he break the news to Vincent? he wondered. How and when would he tell Vincent about his plan to move out? And most importantly how would Vincent react to the news?

He did not have the answers to all those questions. But the problem of Vincent was what worried him the most.

CHAPTER 25

Aryan had not spoken to his mother ever since he had left Kornur for Mumbai. So many months had gone by and he had had absolutely no contact with her. He missed her deeply and he thought about her quite often now especially after he had taken a break from painting.

He was less occupied and less busy now and his days were freer. He had much time to contemplate and think and to dream and relax.

Every afternoon after lunch he would walk to a nearby park and sit on a bench under the shade of a tree and he would think of his mother. He wondered how she was doing and how she was surviving. How was her health now? he would ask himself but he could never answer it. He did not know anything at all. She too had no idea where he lived and what he did. She did not know if he had established himself as an artist yet or not. She did not know if he was even alive or not. She was completely unaware of his very existence just as he was completely unaware of her very existence. He wondered if he would ever get to see her again. He hoped to but he was not so sure about it.

He wished he could contact her just to speak to her or just to write her a little letter. But how could he? He could not. They never had a telephone in their house so how could he call and speak to her? How could he hear her sweet motherly voice? He could not. And she did not know how to read or write so how could he write to her? He could not. It was pointless. All he could do was to think about her and hope that she was doing fine. And that was exactly what he did every day.

Another month passed by. Aryan's schedule had slightly changed now. He still got up at the same time but he did not paint. He instead made breakfast for himself and for Vincent after he finished drinking his tea.

Vincent had taught him how to make an omelet and scrambled eggs and burji and even bull's-eye. Basically all the easy egg dishes. And Aryan had started to enjoy these egg dishes by now especially the way Vincent made them.

He had never had eggs in such different ways before coming to Mumbai. In Kornur people consumed eggs only in two ways. Either they had boiled eggs or they had raw eggs. Nothing else. No omelets or burjis or scrambled eggs or bull's-eyes. Nothing.

And so he found the new styles very fascinating and tasty. He learned to make them very quickly and gradually he took over the breakfast-making department. He also began to improvise and improve upon the method that

Vincent had taught him. Then the two of them would have their breakfast on the dining table.

Vincent understood Aryan's need to take a break but he had also warned him not to stay away from painting for too long for he would then lose the discipline and routine that he had acquired. Aryan agreed with him. An absence of too long would eventually make him too lazy and he did not want that to happen.

After Vincent left for work Aryan would usually watch TV for a couple of hours with a little drawing pad and a pencil in his hand. And all along while he watched he would also draw and make sketches on that little pad of anything and everything and of whatever he felt like drawing or sketching. He only used his pencil and never any colors. That was the closest thing to painting he did now. It kept his mind occupied and distracted.

After his afternoon walks around the area and his thinking sessions at different parks and gardens he would get home by five or six in the evening and then do pretty much nothing at all. He wasted his time in idle thought or he again watched something on TV.

On weekends he would go to Rashid's gallery to look at his paintings displayed up on the walls. He felt proud of himself again. They were not sold yet but they looked good, he thought. He always looked around at the other paintings by other artists, searching for inspiration. But he was exhausted. His well of inspiration was completely drained and dried up and he was waiting for it to fill up again.

Rashid had told him that a few buyers seemed interested in his artworks. They had asked him about the paintings and the artist, he told Aryan. Aryan was delighted to hear that news. But he was not sure if Rashid was just making it up or was he really telling the truth. He could not tell.

If they were so interested why had they not yet purchased the paintings then? he thought but he did not ask Rashid. He could not help but feel that maybe Rashid was lying to him just to keep him motivated and positive and just to give him hope. But he hoped his feelings were misguided this time. He hoped he was wrong.

After Vincent would get back home from work they would either order dinner or go out for it. And by eleven at night Aryan would be off to bed.

He still got up and slept at the same time but his days were less productive now. He followed this routine for another two months.

CHAPTER 26

It had been one whole year now since Aryan had come to Mumbai. Twelve months had just flown by as if it were a fast train passing a small insignificant platform, quick and blurry and formless and uneventful.

Out of the two paintings that Aryan had submitted around three months ago not a single one had been sold yet. And this was bad news. His paintings were threatened now. They were under serious threat of being taken down from the walls to make room for other paintings by other artists. As Rashid had said the previous time, they were taking up valuable space. Space which other artists deserved too, perhaps more than him.

He was aware of that. His career was under threat too. He remembered what Rashid had said to him when he had gone to submit those paintings three months ago. Rashid had said he would keep the paintings on display for about three months. That was what he had said and Aryan had agreed to it too. He had been very confident then but he was not so anymore.

He thought about it a lot and it bothered him

greatly now. What bad luck, he said to himself. The three months that Rashid had promised him had passed by quicker than he had expected. Now what? he wondered. He did not know and he was afraid to find out. He was afraid to go to the gallery now for fear of being given the bad news. He did not wish to meet Rashid. What if Rashid would tell him that both the paintings were going to be taken down immediately? What if Rashid would tell him the same thing as the previous time, "Sorry, Aryan, but it's nothing personal." What would he do then? he asked himself. Again he had no answer.

The hell with all that, he thought. He would not go to the gallery. He would avoid Rashid, he decided. That would not improve the situation but it might save him the pain of finding out the truth. He did not think he could handle the truth again or handle failure again. He did not want the truth now. He wanted hope. He wanted the flickering flame of hope to remain alive within him and the truth from Rashid would completely extinguish that already dying flame. And all he wished to do now was to prolong its death and to stretch it out a little longer, long enough to find new hope.

He knew that the moment he would come to know that his paintings were going to be taken down or were already taken down he would break. He would be shattered and all hope would be lost. As long as he was unaware of the news he would continue to have some hope, he thought. The hope that his paintings were still displayed on the walls of the gallery and that they would sell one day, someday. The truth could not hurt him if he was unaware of it, he thought. And so he resolved to live in denial and remain blissfully unaware. It was very immature of him and he knew that and he preferred it that way.

One afternoon while on his daily walk Aryan passed by a small ill-maintained garden. The gate to the doomed garden was low in height and completely rusted with little patches of black paint from its younger days still showing. But for the most part it was all rusted and worn-down by natural elements.

While he was walking past it he looked over the gate and into the garden. He saw that it was in terrible condition as if it had not been maintained since many years. Trees and plants had grown in there randomly and haphazardly and they were all equally dried up and withered and dusty-brown in color. The garden looked utterly abandoned.

He looked carefully inside trying to figure out if it was ever a garden in the first place. He could not make out. It seemed to have been abandoned years ago. Then through the old dried up trees he saw a little dirt ground in the middle of the compound. He wondered what it was. Maybe children used to play there once upon a time, he thought. Football or cricket maybe or some other silly game of theirs. He smiled as he thought of them playing there. Maybe there was grass there once, he thought, on which people sat peacefully to relax under the late evening sun.

Then he suddenly stopped himself from thinking further. It was such a silly subject to think about, he decided. What use was it to think about such things now? he asked himself. It was of no use at all.

He stepped closer to the gate almost touching it now and he tried to see if he could notice anything else. And he did. He saw the old ruined remains of what must have once been tracks to walk or jog on. He could see it clearly now running between and through the dried up overgrown vegetation in a circle.

He smiled again, proud of his discovery. Then he looked around more carefully holding the rusted gate with his neck stretched out and he saw benches. He saw one, three, five, and then eight benches. It was definitely a garden once, he said to himself and smiled again. He loved gardens, even old dilapidated ones. What a pity, he thought. It must have been a great garden once.

"Hey you! What do you want?" he heard someone shout.

It was a husky voice and it seemed irritated. The voice took him by surprise and he quickly stepped away from the gate. He was afraid to look around and see whom the voice belonged to. He stood there paralyzed, not knowing in which direction to move away.

"You! What do you want here?" the voice asked him again, this time much more clearly.

Aryan turned and looked at the left side of the gate from where the voice seemed to appear. There was a small compact cabin there on the other side of the gate that he had not noticed before. The cabin had a tiny window from which he saw a head peering out and looking at him in anger. It was the face of a young man.

"Are you dumb?" the head asked him. "Can't you speak? What do you want?"

"Nothing," Aryan said loudly. "I don't want anything."

"Then why are you here?" the head said and disappeared inside again.

Aryan still looked at the tiny window and he could only see darkness there now. He heard a door opening on the other side and he started to walk away.

Then the man addressed him again, "Are you here for that job?"

Aryan stopped. He turned around and looked at the man. He finally got to see the man properly and clearly. The man was dressed in an old black uniform that looked like it had not been washed for months. Aryan realized that it was the watchman. He seemed to be in his late thirties but he looked quite young with his clean-shaven face.

"What job?" Aryan asked him.

"You don't know what job you came for?"

"I didn't come for any job."

"Oh, never mind then," the watchman said and turned to walk away from the gate.

"Wait!" Aryan shouted. "What job were you talking about?"

The watchman turned around and looked at Aryan. Then he pointed at the wall next to the gate and said, "Look at that notice there."

Aryan looked at where the watchman had pointed and he saw a white paper stuck to the wall. He went closer to it and he began to read it. The notice said that there was a vacancy for a night watchman for this very abandoned garden. The authorities in charge of protecting the garden had decided to keep a watchman for nights as well and if anyone was interested they could meet the concerned person to discuss the wages and timings. The notice further said that the person applying for the job must be eighteen or above. And at the bottom of the notice the address and phone number of the concerned person were stated.

Aryan looked at the date of the notice and found out that the notice was put up two months ago.

"Is this still valid?" Aryan asked the watchman who had come closer to the gate now.

"Yes," the watchman said. "You are the first person to look at this notice."

"Where's this address?"

"Just five minutes away from here. Walk straight and you will see a building of that name as given in the notice. The boss' office is on the ground floor itself."

"I see," said Aryan. "Is the vacancy only for a night watchman?"

The watchman looked at him suspiciously. Then he said, "Yes. Because I work here during the day. And I don't plan to leave from here anytime soon."

Aryan nodded. There was silence for a few moments. They looked at each other and then Aryan looked away. The watchman continued to look at him. The dry leaves of the trees made a rustling sound in the afternoon wind. Birds chirped here and there. The silence continued.

Aryan knew he had made the watchman angry through no fault of his own. It was obvious. The watchman had felt threatened. He thought Aryan had an evil eye on his day shift and so he wanted to protect it by being rude and intimidating. It was only human nature to do that. It was no one's fault. Aryan quickly walked away from there. The watchman followed him with his eyes.

He followed the watchman's directions and reached the boss' office without any difficulty. The office was on the ground floor itself just as the watchman had told him. He knocked on the door thrice and waited. He could hear someone speaking loudly inside. That was the boss, he thought. He waited till the speaking had stopped and then he knocked again thrice.

"Yes? Come in!" someone shouted.

Aryan opened the door slowly, putting his head in first and then the rest of his body. He entered into a small cramped room which was almost completely occupied by a large table behind which the boss sat. He looked at the man who would be his boss and the man looked back at him with a questioning look on his face. Aryan could see the huge stomach of the man bulging out like it was about to burst. The man had a big round face with barely any hair on his head and a thick line of red powder smeared from between his eyebrows up to the middle of his forehead. He had dark-red betel juice in his mouth.

Aryan told the man that he had come for the night watchman job. The man looked at him and nodded. He could not believe that someone was actually interested in that job.

"Are you above eighteen?" the man asked.

"Yes sir," Aryan replied.

The man nodded. He did not ask for any proof.

"So let me tell you the reason first," the man started with the red juice still in his mouth. "The reason we have decided to keep a night watchman is because there have been many complaints about a bunch of juvenile delinquents entering the garden at night, every night, by climbing over the gate to smoke and drink inside. Sometimes they even take drugs over there. And they used to do the same in the daytime as well, you see."

Aryan nodded.

"But once we appointed a watchman they stopped coming. So now we want to appoint a watchman for the night as well so they will stop coming then."

The man bent down and spat the red juice into a steel container. Then he drank some water from a plastic bottle that was kept on the table.

"Do you think you can do it?" the man asked.

"Yes. But what do I have to do?"

"Just lock the gate from the other side and sit there in the cabin or somewhere near the gate. Once they know you are there they will not climb over."

"And if they do?"

"They won't. They are stupid little teenage kids. They get scared because they know they are doing something wrong, you see. And you will be armed with a stick. If they climb over you can hit them with it."

The man laughed after saying that and his big soft stomach wiggled. Aryan looked at his stomach and then he looked up again so as not to get caught looking at it. The man stopped laughing and his stomach stopped wiggling. He coughed and cleared his throat and then he drank some more water.

Then he said, "You can also scold them. Shout at them not to come back again. Tell them you will call the police."

Aryan did not respond. He stared at the man with wide eyes. Call the police? This job was riskier than he had imagined, he thought. The man looked at him. He had seen Aryan's face change instantly. He smiled at Aryan.

"Of course you won't have to actually do it," the man said. "So don't worry."

Aryan immediately relaxed. His eyes were normal again. He smiled.

"Your timing will be from seven in the evening to seven in the morning, every day, no holidays."

Aryan was taken aback. Twelve hours? What would he sit there and do for twelve hours straight that too at night? he asked himself. That was too much for him, he said to himself. He could not do it. That was impossible.

The man was looking at him. Aryan looked down at the big table in front of him. His palms were getting sweaty and he wiped them on his pants.

"Any problem?" the man asked.

Aryan started thinking now. And he thought quickly. What other choice did he have? he thought. Nothing. What else could he do? He could do nothing else. Either take it or leave it. Could he get a job somewhere else? he wondered. No. He could not. He knew he could not. This was the only job that did not require any particular skill as such and he had come across it by pure chance as if it were meant for him and him only. As if an angel had guided him to that rotten gate and ruined garden. It was meant to be, he said to himself. In his desperation he sensed fate's hand in it. He had mistaken sheer coincidence for a miracle. He was that desperate.

"No sir," Aryan said.

The man informed him that his salary would be seven thousand rupees per month. Aryan nodded in agreement. Then he started thinking again. Would seven thousand be enough to rent his own place? he thought. He was not so sure. He had not yet searched for any place to stay. He did not mind where it was or how bad it was as long as it was cheap. How could he find cheap accommodation? he wondered. Where would he even start searching? Then it struck him.

He told the man he needed a cheap place to stay, a place whose rent he could afford with the salary he would earn. Where could he find such a place? he asked the man.

The man thought for some time. Then he said, "I'm not sure I know any place as such. But I can do you a favor. There's a shed in that abandoned garden at the back. It's small but it's empty. And it's made of concrete. At least you can have a solid roof over your head."

Aryan smiled. He became excited but he tried not to show too much of it.

"You can stay for free over there," the man said. "At least it will be used that way. But I warn you it's nothing great."

Aryan's smile became broader now. Free accommodation? That was amazing, he said to himself. Then he reminded himself to keep calm and not to show his excitement although it was getting very difficult to do that now.

The man informed him that there was a toilet

next to the shed too. He also promised to provide Aryan with a mattress and a pillow and a stove for cooking.

Aryan was delighted and he thanked the man. Since it was a Friday the man asked him to join from Monday. Aryan gladly agreed and left.

He walked away from there feeling elated and happy. He was excited. He could not believe his luck. He got a place to stay for free. It could not get any better than this, he thought. He had hit the jackpot.

The job would be terribly boring and he was aware of that. He would also have to stay away from painting for a while and he knew that too. He had no illusions about his situation. None whatsoever. Until his two paintings did not sell he could not go back to painting, he said to himself. He needed that money to continue painting and to buy new materials.

He still had hope that his paintings would sell one day and he hoped that day would come by soon. But painting would have to wait for it was all about survival now.

Aryan had to now undertake the most difficult task he faced. The one task he absolutely dreaded. The one obstacle he had feared. It was the task of breaking this news to Vincent and convincing him.

The next morning during breakfast Aryan finally spoke to Vincent about moving out. Vincent was taken aback by this sudden development.

Aryan explained it to him in detail carefully and politely. He had to move out, he told Vincent. He must survive on his own now. It was important for him, he said. It must be done. He pleaded with Vincent to understand him.

Vincent said nothing. He looked at Aryan without saying a word, barely blinking. Aryan looked back at him. There was silence. Neither spoke. Vincent still looked at him and then he looked down at his plate.

Aryan remained silent too. He allowed the news to sink in. He gave Vincent some time to process it. Then he went on to give more reasons as to why he must leave. They were valid ones, he said. Vincent nodded.

It was imperative for his growth, he said. Vincent nodded again. He seemed to understand but he chose not to speak yet. Aryan understood his need for silence.

For a few minutes the dead silence remained hanging in the air and in the room and in the house, stiff and heavy and tangible.

"And what about painting?" Vincent asked.

"I will wait till those two paintings are sold and then I will use the money to start again."

"And what if they never sell?"

"They will. I have hope," Aryan said.

Vincent smiled. Then he nodded without looking at Aryan. For the first time Aryan was the one looking Vincent in the face and Vincent was looking away.

"You have hope," Vincent said. "That's good. Hope is important."

"I have to do this," Aryan said with conviction.

Vincent did not reply. He was looking at his plate and smiling. He looked at Aryan and then he looked away again. He knew Aryan was right and what he said was true.

"I know," Vincent said.

Aryan did not respond immediately. He waited for a few moments. Silence returned to the dining table. Aryan took a bite of his bread and omelet and chewed it slowly and swallowed it. He looked at Vincent. Vincent was looking at the floor now. He had taken just one bite of his bread and omelet.

"You are right," said Vincent.

He looked at Aryan and nodded gently. Then he smiled and said, "I'm proud of you, Aryan."

Aryan nodded in gratitude. He knew everything would be fine now. He felt relaxed and relieved. Vincent was convinced now. The main obstacle had been overcome successfully and the main task completed. He felt at ease and his heavy heart grew lighter.

They finished their breakfast and then they went and settled down on the sofa to continue their discussion. The discussion was not yet over, just the difficult part of it was. Vincent had a few questions still and Aryan was ready to answer them all. Even though Vincent was convinced he was still concerned about the whole idea.

"What about your paintings in Rashid's gallery?" Vincent asked Aryan. "Any news?"

"No. Not yet," said Aryan.

"Three months are over. Did he take them down by now?"

"I don't know. I haven't visited the gallery for that reason."

"You are afraid he has," said Vincent.

"Yes."

"That's foolish. You can't live like that. You have to know."

"Not knowing about it is the only reason I still have hope."

Vincent shook his head. He looked at Aryan and he could see that Aryan really believed not knowing the truth would benefit him.

"You can't just run away from the truth like this," Vincent said. "It doesn't work that way. Is your hope dependent only on the fate of those two paintings?"

"I think so," Aryan said.

"That's bad, Aryan. Hope is something you must always possess, regardless of the truth. And for how long do you plan to live in such ignorance?"

Aryan did not answer. He did not have an answer, not even a wrong one or a petty one. He knew Vincent was right. For how long could he keep up with this act? he asked himself and he had no answer. It was almost as if Vincent had read his mind and had asked him the very question he could not answer. Vincent looked at him intently.

"Do you want me to talk to Rashid?" Vincent asked.

"No," Aryan said.

"So if those two paintings never sell you will never paint again?"

"Not until I can afford it on my own," said Aryan. "If I can earn enough money to start painting again and buy new paints and canvases and everything else then I will start again. But I must do it on my own."

Vincent was satisfied with Aryan's answer. It was a perfectly valid one and he could understand the young man's need to do it on his own and to not depend on someone else even if that someone was like his father.

Vincent remembered how he was when he was Aryan's age. He too had that intense desire to make it on his own and to prove himself worthy. Worthy of what he did not know and he was sure Aryan did not know either. Worthy of respect or success or maybe of the money one earns.

He too had the same desire to achieve it all independently with no help and no assistance and with only his skills and faith at his disposal and nothing else. No favors or no special treatment, just him against the world striving to achieve something with the whole world in between acting as an invincible obstacle. He could see it clearly now. Aryan was very much like how he was once.

He saw in Aryan the same drive and desire to survive on his own no matter how difficult it was and no matter how impossible or dangerous it was. That desire was stubborn and strong and incurable. It did not just vanish. It did not just go away. It stayed and persisted and thrived unless one turned into an utterly defeated man who had lost all hope and had given up on life completely. But until then that desire existed within one and it troubled one and it troubled one's peace and one's very spirit. And that desire had to be fulfilled. There was no other way around it. It had to be satisfied and then and only then would one be satisfied and one's spirit would be satisfied in turn. That was how it worked.

He had already done it. His spirit was satisfied and his desire fulfilled. Now it was Aryan's turn to do the same.

Vincent looked at Aryan now. Aryan seemed to be thinking something. He had a frown on his face and he looked a little troubled.

"I agree," Vincent said softly. "You are right. You need to do this. Just like I needed to do it once. It must be done."

Aryan looked up at him. He was surprised by Vincent's remark. Vincent put his hand on Aryan's shoulder and squeezed it. Then he smiled.

"And what about Rashid then?" Aryan asked.

"Don't worry, I won't ask him. And neither must you. Keep that little hope you have left and keep it safe. Protect it. You will need it now more than ever."

Aryan smiled. He felt happier now. He felt better about himself and his situation. It was not all bleak and scary. He could see some light now, a silver lining. And he desperately needed to see that light. It was not all bleak, he said to himself.

Then Vincent asked Aryan how he would get a job. Aryan informed him that he had already found one as a night watchman at an abandoned garden. Vincent was surprised and slightly taken aback. He looked at Aryan doubtfully and he tried to read his face but his face was smiling. One could never ascertain a lie from a person's face when a smile was pure and genuine, Vincent thought. It was impossible.

Aryan told Vincent he was serious and then he went on to describe how he had got the job and all the details of it. Vincent was amused by it all. He laughed and Aryan joined him.

"If you are happy then I'm happy," Vincent told Aryan.

Aryan nodded and said, "I'm happy, even though I know it's nothing great."

"You have to start somewhere, don't you? Might as well make the best of it," Vincent said.

Aryan smiled. He felt good. That was exactly what he was looking for, words of encouragement. He wanted someone to tell him that it was fine and it was good and that it was not a big deal. He wanted someone to tell him to make the best of what he had. And Vincent had done just that. He was calm now.

"When does your work start?" Vincent asked.

"Monday evening."

"Alright," said Vincent. "We have one whole day together tomorrow. And I don't have to work. Let's make some more memories together."

"I'm ready," Aryan said and smiled.

"Good," Vincent said, and then he went to get ready for work.

CHAPTER 27

The following day Aryan and Vincent decided to go to watch a cricket match in the stadium. It was a surprise and Aryan was completely unaware of it until that morning.

Vincent had managed to get tickets for a domestic cricket match and he was very excited to let Aryan know about it. But he had controlled himself the previous night as he wanted to surprise Aryan in the morning during breakfast.

And it worked. Aryan was taken aback when he learned what Vincent had in store for him. This was definitely going to be memorable, Aryan thought. He was going to watch his first live cricket match ever. He had never expected this day to come. He was thrilled like a child and Vincent was very happy to see him that way. Vincent was proud of his decision.

After a year in Mumbai Aryan had turned into a die-hard cricket fan just like millions of other Indians. He had never known or realized the importance of cricket among Indians before coming to Mumbai. Kornur had felt like a whole other country when he got to know and experience the craze for cricket. No such craze or fanaticism existed in Kornur. None at all. He had only heard of cricket there but he had never seen any matches before. His only experience with cricket in Kornur was the sight of school children playing it in the evenings after school. And in that too they rarely had an actual ball or bat to play with. The children there used small wooden planks or thick coconut tree branches as bats and small dried-up coconuts as balls. And they looked very content with that equipment. It was normal for them and they never dreamt of having a proper bat or ball. For them that was cricket.

But even so cricket was not a very popular sport in Kornur. It was just another sport they played when they could not play football for in Kornur football had a much greater importance among the children and the youth, not cricket. Football was the poor man's sport. They had to afford just one football and if they could not do that then they usually played with a small coconut whose shell had become comparatively soft. And if that too was not possible then they searched for a plastic bottle and filled it with a little water to make it heavy enough to play with.

Football was loved and played by everyone there. And some had even claimed to have seen a match or two which was highly doubtful. It was more of a myth. But many had claimed to have heard football matches on the radio and there were so many of them who claimed it that it might as well be true.

But Aryan had never heard such claims about cricket. No one had claimed to have seen a cricket match and no one had ever claimed to have heard one on the radio. Not once had he heard anyone do that. And he wondered why it was so.

How was Kornur so different from the rest of India regarding such an important thing as cricket? he wondered. How was that even possible? How could a village be so different in likes and thoughts when it was part of one and the same country? He did not know. He had no idea Kornur was so different until he came to Mumbai. He smiled when he thought of how different his village was from the rest of India. He liked it that way. He liked its isolation and sometimes its ignorance too.

Kornur seemed so innocent to him when compared to the rest of India. He liked its innocence. There was something inherently pure about his village and its people too, he thought. They were so simple and so naïve and innocent just like their village. Was it the village that defined its people or was it the people that defined their village? he wondered. Did a village take on the traits and characteristics of its people or was it the other way around? Who influenced whom? he thought. Maybe they both influenced each other. Who knew? he said to himself.

Kornur was so naive, he thought. Kornur was like a child that had been sheltered for so long that it could not survive in the real world for it was not used to it as it was not raised in that environment.

His village was very simple and ignorant and its people were the same but there was something very pure and beautiful and appealing about it just like there was something very pure and beautiful and appealing about everything that was naive and ignorant and simple and innocent. It was something that was irresistible. It was something that could not be explained and that should not be explained.

On coming to Mumbai Aryan had quickly realized the significance of cricket in India. For the first time he was able to witness the mood of the entire nation from Mumbai. The city gave him that opportunity. He saw that very few things united the country the way cricket did. For all its diversity it seemed as if the country could only come together and be held together by that sport. Sometimes it felt as if cricket was the glue that kept it together.

It was all so fascinating for him. It was marvelous. Cricket was like a religion. It was an addiction. The players were thrown up to the status of Gods and Demi-Gods. They were no longer allowed to be human beings. It was mandatory. The people never allowed them to stay humans. Not a chance.

And it seemed to Aryan as if only Kornur had missed out on this great ride, on this giant wheel of cricket. It was weird, he thought, but it was truly fascinating. He wondered what made cricket so special over all the other sports? Why only cricket got such attention and such devotion and such worship? Why not football or basketball or athletics or tennis or badminton or hockey or any other sport?

Why not hockey? he wondered. Was not hockey the national sport of India? As far as he could remember that was what he was taught at school. Maybe in that too Kornur was behind the trend. Maybe the national sport had been changed to cricket. Or maybe there was no national sport anymore. It was best if there was no particular sport considered the national sport, he thought. That way all sports would be considered to be equal and that was how it should be.

Anyway there was no point in asking such redundant questions, he said to himself. What would he achieve by that? Nothing at all. He himself had become a cricket fanatic within twelve short months. He loved the sport now. He loved watching it and listening to it. He loved talking about it and he did it passionately. He gave his opinions on it firmly and assertively. He argued on it as if it were an important political discussion. The ignorant boy from Kornur had become one of the millions now.

And that was why he was so excited to go and watch the match live in a stadium and Vincent had known quite well he would be. It did not matter what match it was or who was playing against whom. It was the experience that mattered, the sheer thrill of sitting in a stadium with other fanatics enjoying the game. That was why Vincent had chosen it as the going-away present.

The match was between Mumbai and Baroda and it was in South Mumbai. It was going to start at nine-thirty in the morning and so they left the house by eight in Vincent's car and they reached the stadium by nine. Since it was a Sunday morning there was no traffic at all and they reached well on time.

Both were excited now. They bought soft drinks and some snacks and then they settled down at their seats. It was going to be a long but pleasant day. The match began and they watched it intently. They cheered and jeered along with the rest of the crowd even though they supported no team in particular. Of course Mumbai being the home team had more support from the crowd. But Aryan and Vincent did not care. They were there to enjoy themselves and to make new memories and to cement old ones. They cheered for both teams with the same enthusiasm and they jeered at both with the same enthusiasm as well. They were supporting cricket on this day.

The match lasted for almost six hours. By late evening they were out of the stadium and on their way to have pizza. Vincent took Aryan to a pizza place he had always been very fond of. Aryan had eaten pizza only once before when Vincent had ordered it at home during his first days in Mumbai, and he remembered very well that he had liked it. But this was the first time he was going to a pizza joint. Vincent took him to a place that he claimed was the best pizza joint in the whole of Mumbai.

After they were done eating Aryan agreed with Vincent. His stomach was overfull and he sat still in his chair. Vincent looked at him bewildered for he was equally stuffed and he too sat still in his chair. Both of them could not move for a while.

"It was great," Aryan said with difficulty. "I'm going to miss this."

"I bet you will," Vincent said and smiled. "You must come to meet me every weekend at least since you will be so close. We can have this every weekend."

Aryan smiled but said nothing. He loosened up his belt and then he opened up his pant button. Then he felt much better. He could breathe better now and his stomach had some more room to move. He relaxed on the chair. Vincent looked dazed and tired but he kept on smiling.

"I will," Aryan finally said. "But not to have this. I'm done with pizza for a long while. I feel like vomiting now."

"That happens," Vincent said casually. "That's how you know you have enjoyed it."

"Are you sure? Because it doesn't feel that way."

"I'm very sure."

"Are you in the same dilemma?" Aryan asked.

"Always," said Vincent, and then they both laughed together.

It was already eight by the time they decided to leave for home. They sat in the car and started for home.

They both felt terribly uneasy and nauseous. After sometime while driving Vincent asked Aryan, "Are you feeling uneasy too?"

"Very much," Aryan said quickly. "And you?"

"I feel terrible," Vincent said. "Do you want to have some cool fresh air?"

"Yes please," Aryan said, closing his eyes in discomfort.

Vincent immediately turned away from the direction of his house and headed toward the seafront of Mumbai.

On reaching there they went and sat down on the huge tetrapods lying on the beach and they faced the immense Arabian Sea ahead. The sea was dark and fidgety and the waves dashed against the big concrete tetrapods way below them making that pleasant sound that soothes the mind and the spirit.

The cool heavy sea breeze blew vigorously against their bodies and their hair and clothes flew back with the oncoming force in the direction of the blowing wind. They squinted and looked far ahead into the immense mass of restless black water and they searched for the horizon in vain.

They found nothing and they saw nothing. But they felt and experienced something. They felt the cool wind hitting against them in the darkness and the spray of little drops of salty sea water falling on them after the waves struck the giant tetrapods. They felt calm and relaxed and they felt burdenless and painless. They were devoid of sadness and worries then. They felt blissful and invincible.

They did not speak much for words would ruin the sanctity of the place and the moment. Words would not be able to capture the mood and the moment and the sanctity of it all. Words could never do that. They had never possessed the ability to do that. They were not capable enough. Only feelings and silence were capable and they were all that mattered at such a moment.

They felt easy now, the uneasiness draining out of them in the silence and in the darkness silently and quietly. They breathed in the cool sea air and they found new life and new peace. And they were completely at peace now with anything and everything. They sat there in the same place for more than an hour and then they walked along the beach for another half an hour. Then they decided to head back to the car to go back home.

By the time they reached home it was past eleven. They were both very tired and sleepy. They had had a long day and they deserved some rest. By eleven-thirty both of them were fast asleep in their respective rooms.

CHAPTER 28

Monday had finally arrived. It was Aryan's last day at Vincent's house. His work was going to start now and he was already mentally prepared. He was excited.

He packed his clothes and all other essential things in the morning and he kept them ready in the living room. As always all his belongings comfortably fit into one suitcase. He never had many possessions anyway and he preferred to pack only the ones that were necessary for most of the time he would have to wear the watchman's uniform that would be given to him.

He had decided to leave the extra clothes at the house itself. Vincent was more than happy to let Aryan do that for that provided him with additional hope that Aryan would keep visiting him on a regular basis. The thought of that comforted him.

Aryan had also decided to leave behind all his paintings and painting materials at the house. Obviously he could not take all of that to his new accommodation, he thought. Vincent was glad again and he supported Aryan's decision. It made a lot of sense, he told Aryan. That was another thing that gave him hope of Aryan's return.

Aryan decided to leave the house for the garden by six in the evening. He would take at least fifteen minutes to reach there by rickshaw. He wanted to be early on his first day to make an impression. Before leaving for work Vincent promised Aryan that he would return before Aryan left. Aryan said he did not have to do that but Vincent insisted. Aryan relented. Then Vincent left for work.

Aryan spent the rest of the day in front of the TV doing pretty much nothing at all. He watched some news, something he rarely did, and then he quickly got bored and moved on to a music channel. Finally as he always did he ended up watching the repeat of an old cricket match. When would he get to see it again? he wondered. He did not know exactly. Maybe on Sunday afternoons when he would come to the house.

He wondered how his life was going to change now. No holidays and so no point of weekends. Had he mentioned that to Vincent? he asked himself. Had he informed Vincent that he had no holidays and no weekends as such? No. He had not. He forgot.

How could he forget? he thought. How stupid of him. Vincent would probably be so excited thinking about those weekends, he thought. Vincent looked so happy when he spoke about the weekends. And now he would be so disappointed.

He should have mentioned it at the pizza joint itself, he said to himself.

Now what could he do? Nothing. There was nothing he could do now other than disappoint Vincent during the weekends. The only time he would get to visit Vincent was on Sunday afternoons after he had slept for at least five or six hours after his duty. And then he would have to go back to work in the evening again. That was going to be his life from now on, he thought.

He could easily visit Vincent every afternoon but Vincent only took a holiday on Sundays. That was the only day Vincent was free. So Sunday afternoons it was, he decided.

Then he turned his attention back to the match. For now all he wanted to do was to watch as much cricket as possible for he would not be able to do this very often from now on. His luxurious days were coming to an end.

As promised Vincent got back home before Aryan could leave. It was six in the evening now and Aryan was all set to leave. He picked up his suitcase and the two of them went down together. Vincent was emotional. Aryan was expecting it. Looking at Vincent even Aryan became emotional.

They barely spoke while they waited for a rickshaw. The whole matter was so silly, Aryan thought. They were getting emotional for nothing at all. But he was sad too. He could not deny it for the sadness was all over his face. It had hit him suddenly out of nowhere and he was not prepared for it. He understood it now. It was not the physical distance between them that Vincent was so worried about. Not at all. It had absolutely nothing to do with physical distance. It was the emotional distance that would inevitably come between the two of them that Vincent was worried about.

Vincent had known it since before. He knew it very well. He knew that nothing would be the same as before. It would all change, first slightly and then drastically. Emotional distance was bound to appear between them. It always did without fail. It was the rule of life. And when emotional distance was in question then physical distance did not matter at all. It had nothing to do with being twenty minutes away. Two people could be sitting right next to each other and there could still be a great distance between them that could not be bridged or traveled.

That was a fact of life and Vincent knew it all along. It was only Aryan who had just realized it. That was why Vincent wanted to come home early, Aryan thought. To bid him farewell like a father would to his son, man to man.

Aryan smiled. He felt so foolish now. He was still a kid, he told himself. He was still immature. He still had a lot to learn in life and he was not even halfway there yet.

The road was crowded and noisy but the traffic was not so bad. It was slowly getting darker now. All the rickshaws that came by were already occupied. Vincent walked over to the other side of the road in the hope of finding a rickshaw and Aryan kept trying to find one from the same place in front of the building gate. It was Vincent who succeeded at catching one and Aryan crossed over to the other side of the road.

Vincent stood there with his hand on the roof of the rickshaw. He was smiling now. It was a pleasant one, not a sad one. His smile conveyed happiness and pride as if he had finally convinced himself that everything would be fine and everything would be great.

But Aryan was not smiling now. His face was serious and he looked nervous. His heart was pounding faster and faster. His palms were sweaty again. He looked at Vincent. Vincent was still smiling at him. Both said nothing.

The rickshaw driver looked at them in silence wondering what was going on. He was afraid to speak up. In spite of all the noise around them there was complete silence for a few moments.

Finally the rickshaw driver got fed up and broke the silence. "Where do you want to go?" he asked them in an irritated tone.

Aryan looked at the driver. He struggled to remember the address as he was caught off-guard for a brief moment. Then he told the driver where he wanted to go. The driver ordered him to sit in the rickshaw with just a quick sideways nod of his head.

"It's time," Vincent said and placed his hand on Aryan's shoulder.

"Yes," Aryan said and embraced Vincent. Vincent embraced him back.

"Don't cry now," Vincent said teasingly. "I will see you on the weekends."

Aryan suddenly remembered and told Vincent that he had no holidays. He told him what he had decided. But Vincent's face did not change. His smile remained intact.

"It's fine," Vincent said. "Sunday afternoons it is."

Aryan nodded and then bent down and entered the rickshaw. The rickshaw driver was relieved. Vincent and Aryan said goodbye to each other and then the rickshaw started away.

CHAPTER 29

Almost twenty hours later around five in the evening Aryan's train arrived at Kornur station.

He looked out the window and became excited. He got down from the train and stretched his thin body and then he yawned a long yawn. He took in a deep breath of the fresh and clean and pure fish-smelling air of Kornur and instantly felt the difference in the air.

He relaxed. The difference was marked and obvious. The air here was not polluted like the air in Mumbai. It was cool and breathable. He took another deep breath and then another and another until the smell of the cool fish-smelling air had finally satisfied him.

He felt as if he had come back to a place where he had always belonged. This was home, he said to himself. He had never realized until now how much he had missed Kornur. The silence was so contrary to Mumbai. The station was not crowded or chaotic at all but empty and peaceful.

Whatever he saw around him and compared felt as if it was much better here than it had been in Mumbai. His entire view and attitude toward

Kornur had changed completely. Kornur felt like heaven now, like a beautiful little paradise. He was excited to be back and he could not wait to reach home and see his mother. He could not wait to surprise her.

He walked out of the station and caught a rickshaw and fifteen minutes later he arrived at his neighborhood. He asked the rickshaw driver to stop and then he paid the driver and got out of the rickshaw.

He stood there and looked around with a big smile on his face. It was all exactly the same, he thought. Nothing had changed at all. He ran toward his home, smiling and laughing all along like a small kid coming back home from school.

People from his neighborhood recognized him. "Isn't that Aryan?" "Is that really him?" they whispered amongst themselves. But lost in his happiness he failed to notice the sad and tense expression on their faces when they saw him. They did not smile or welcome him with enthusiasm and they all had a look of deep concern.

Aryan reached his house and stopped. He looked at the house and then he bent forward slightly and placed his palms on his knees and panted heavily for a few seconds. Then he stood up straight and looked at the house again. As far as he could remember it looked exactly the same as on the day he had left. No difference at all. But it looked a little messier and unkempt from the outside than he could remember.

He went and knocked on the door. "Ma!" he shouted. "Open the door Ma! I'm back!"

There was no response. He was so happy he kept on laughing and smiling. He waited for her to open the door but she did not. Then he knocked on the door again and called out, "Ma! Are you there?"

He got no response. Maybe she was at the market, he thought. He gave up and turned around and when he did so he saw people gathering around him. There were already a dozen people assembled and among them he recognized Raja and Ramesh. They were standing in silence and looking at him with the same expression on their faces as the rest of the crowd.

He looked back at them and then at the others. He wondered what was happening. Why were all these people looking at him in this way? he asked himself.

He walked slowly over to Raja and Ramesh. They quickly looked down, avoiding eye contact with him. He stopped in front of them and waited. They said nothing. He tried to catch their eyes but they did not let him. The dreadful silence became unbearable.

"What's wrong?" Aryan finally asked them.

They looked up at him and then they looked down again. But they did not answer him. He looked at Raja and held him by the shoulders. Raja avoided his gaze as he had done once before years ago.

"What the hell is happening over here?" Aryan asked irritated.

And this time Ramesh replied and his reply was a straightforward one. "She's no more, son," he said, and then he said nothing further.

Ramesh's reply took him by surprise. He was left speechless. He could not believe those words. He sat down on the ground in front of all those curious eyes. His eyes narrowed. His palms grew sweaty. He repeated what he had just heard but with no voice to support it. He began breathing heavily now and he continued to mouth Ramesh's reply again and again and every time he repeated it the words became more and more audible and once it turned into a whisper he suddenly stopped repeating it. And then the words sunk in and they finally attained some meaning in his turbulent mind. They made sense now. His mother was dead.

Ramesh knelt down on the ground next to him and he placed his hand on his back.

"She died six months ago after suffering from some serious illness for almost a year," Ramesh said, and then he stopped and waited for a reaction.

Aryan did not react. Then Ramesh continued, "She had no idea what the illness was and so she ignored it for a long time thinking it would go away on its own sooner or later. By the time she consulted a doctor it was already too late to do anything. Even the doctor failed to point out what it was. There was nothing anyone could do to save her, son. Nothing. It was too late."

Ramesh stopped talking. He gently rubbed his hand across Aryan's back. Aryan looked at the ground but said nothing.

"We tried to get in touch with you when we came to know about her illness," Ramesh said. "We knew her days were numbered and we tried to contact you so that you could come home and be with her when she took her last breath."

Aryan did not say anything. He barely reacted. He did not shed a single tear in front of all those people watching him. He looked blankly at the ground.

Ramesh stood up and put his hand in his shirt pocket and brought out a key. After the funeral Ramesh had safely kept the keys to Aryan's house hoping that he would come back one day. That day had finally arrived now.

Ramesh handed over the keys to Aryan. Aryan put out his hand and took it mechanically. He still did not say anything. He stood up and turned around and then he walked slowly toward the door of his house. He opened it and went inside, dragging his suitcase behind him. Then he shut the door.

Once he was inside the house and away from the inquisitive eyes of all those people he let out all his emotions with a scream of despair. He cried and cursed himself again and again. He had no one in his life now, he thought. No father or mother or family. He was all alone now and he had nothing and nobody to live for anymore.

Life was so cruel, he said to himself. Whenever we felt like things were finally going our way and when everything good was happening to us and when we would find happiness at last, just then life would interfere and knock us down and put us back in our place where we belonged, hopeless and helpless and at its mercy.

Life did not want us to be constantly happy. It hated our happiness and it was obvious, he thought. Why else would it deal with us in such a terrible manner? It could not bear our happiness. It liked to make us suffer. It gave us hope just so that it could snatch it away from us in an instant. In an instant when we required it the most.

And there was no point in fighting against it for life was always victorious. It always won without exception. And it had won once again. Life had finally defeated him.

Was his life really worth living now? he wondered. For whom did he have to live now? For what purpose? What was the point of going on with this miserable life that kept on disappointing him? Or maybe he was the one who kept on disappointing life, he thought.

He felt guilty for her death. It was his fault, he told himself. Whose fault could it be if not his? No one's. He was the only one to be blamed and so he blamed himself. He had no obligations anymore. None at all. But oddly enough he felt more burdened by this fact than liberated.

He went to the cupboard and searched around. He found what he was looking for, a bed sheet. He could not live with this guilt for the rest of his life. It was only because of him that his mother had died, he thought again. How could he ever forgive himself for this? he asked himself. He could not. He could never forgive himself for this and he knew that quite well. It would be easier to just take his own life, he thought.

He tied the bed sheet into a noose and hung it from the ceiling fan. Then he took the only chair that was in the house and placed it right under the fan. He had to end his life, he thought again. There was no other choice. No other way around it. Everything was ready. Preparations being done all he had to do now was execute.

He was terribly nervous. He decided to sit down for some time to calm his nerves and muster up enough courage to actually commit the act. He sat down on the floor still as a rock while tears gently washed down his cheeks. The floor was cool and the air in the room warm. Outside it was hot. His face was oily and sticky with sweat and his heart was beating rapidly. His hands were trembling and his palms were sweaty. His eyes were blood-red and watery and his vision blurred. His warm tears rolled down his cheeks onto his hands and shirt and then onto the cool floor.

The news of her death had numbed his senses and paralyzed his ability to think. He could vividly hear the chaotic noises coming in from the market near his house. He could hear the hustling and bustling of the people outside, the customers trying their best to bargain with the vendors and the vendors trying their best to avoid the bargaining. He could hear it all and he could hear it as if the noises were coming from inside his own head.

It was almost six in the evening. The orange sun was setting for the day on the faraway horizon. The setting sun gave the sky an orangish color which instilled a very lonely feeling within him. But the house gave him a warm and comfortable feeling. A little too comfortable a feeling considering the act he was about to carry out.

The cool floor on which he sat was slowly getting warmer now and he was crying in the most detached manner. He closed his eyes. It felt warm and pleasant but the tears continued to escape through his shut eyelids. He tried to calm himself down by taking deep deliberate breaths. It worked. His hands steadied. His heart slowed down. He stayed still. The noises from the world outside did not seem to distract him nor bother him.

CHAPTER 30

Aryan's eyes opened up and he looked around him. He was a little dazed and his vision was blurry again. He rubbed his eyes vigorously and they slowly cleared up. His vision became clear now and he got back to his senses. Spit drooled out from the side of his mouth and down to his chin and he wiped it away with the back of his palm.

It was dark inside except for a little light seeping in through the window. The room was cool and so was the floor. He was still sitting down on the floor in the same position.

He looked down and he felt his eyes closing up again. He immediately looked up straight. In front of him he could see the chair placed right under the fan and the bed sheet tied into a noose hanging casually from the ceiling fan.

He had fallen asleep while trying to calm his nerves and gather up enough courage and it had saved his life. He stood up unsteadily and searched for the time. The clock was not working. He slowly walked over to the open window and stood there motionless and looked out.

He looked at the rising sun and figured it was

around six in the morning. He had slept for almost twelve hours.

He remained standing there, still looking outside. He was greeted by the cool refreshing sea breeze that gently brushed across his face. It was a pleasant feeling. He felt calm and relaxed now. He felt like the sea breeze had brought back some long-lost peace from someplace far away.

He thought about his mother and it seemed as if he had already recovered from that initial shock. He was emotionally stable now. He was at peace.

He turned around and looked at the suicide apparatus which he had prepared for himself. He thought about what he had planned to do last evening and he could not believe it. He had been so close to killing himself and a flimsy phenomenon like sleep had been his savior.

He turned around and looked outside the window again. The sun was already higher up than before and its rays hit him directly in the eyes. The sea breeze continued to blow his way. He smiled gently. Then he smelled his shirt, it was stinking. He needed a bath, he thought, and then he turned around and walked toward the bathroom.

He had a slow cold bath that lasted for almost thirty minutes and then he felt much better. He got ready in his old clothes and left for Raja's house. He did not have anything to eat as he was not hungry yet.

It was almost seven now. He walked toward

Raja's house in the cold morning through the narrow streets slowly and patiently as if he had all the time in the world. The streets were not much crowded but swarms of fishermen walked about performing their daily routine. He looked all around while walking like a tourist would do and at last he arrived at Raja's house.

He went to the door and knocked on it. He waited for a few moments but no one opened it. He knocked again and again until he heard some movement inside the house. Raja opened the door with squinted eyes, still half asleep and wearing nothing but a lungi. He stared at Aryan with some difficulty and in partial disbelief, surprised to see him at such an hour.

Aryan smiled at him and said, "Good Morning."

"Aryan? We were worried about you–" Raja began to speak but Aryan interrupted him before he could complete.

"Can you take me to Ma's grave, please?" Aryan said.

Raja nodded. "Come in," he told Aryan, opening the door wide for him to enter.

Within ten minutes Raja was ready to go. They walked in complete silence throughout the way in a comfortable pace with Raja in front and Aryan quietly following him right behind. They reached the grave and stopped. Raja looked at Aryan and gave him a slight nod to indicate to him that it was the right grave.

Aryan nodded at Raja in return and then he

knelt down beside the grave and spoke to his mother as if she were present there before him in pure flesh and blood. Raja stood next to Aryan in utter silence with his head held down to his chest and his eyes shut.

Aryan spoke to his mother from the deep recesses of his heart. He told her about everything he had done and about everything he had gone through in Mumbai. He apologized to her for the way he had behaved and he apologized to her for having ignored her. And most importantly he apologized to her for not being there when she needed him the most toward the end of her life and for not being there by her side when she took her last breath.

He did not cry at all. Not a single tear. He knew his mother would not like to see him cry. She would like to see him smiling, he knew that. She was watching him now at this very moment and he was sure of it. Then he sat down by her grave in complete silence. Raja came and sat down beside him.

"I'm sorry for your loss, Aryan," Raja said softly.

Aryan looked at Raja and smiled at him. Then he put his hand over Raja's shoulder and said, "Thanks, Raja. It means a lot."

Raja smiled a short and small smile in return. The two of them sat there for more than an hour without speaking to each other and then they got up to leave. Before leaving the grave Aryan thanked her for all the sacrifices she had made for him, something he would never be able to make up for or repay, he told her.

Aryan and Raja left the grave and started walking back home. They walked halfway back in silence and then suddenly Aryan stopped and looked at Raja. Looking at him even Raja stopped walking.

"Did she suffer a lot?" Aryan asked Raja.

Raja looked at Aryan and realized that it was an important question for him. And Raja understood its importance. He understood why Aryan had asked him this question. Aryan looked at Raja with a hopeless look on his face.

"No. Not at all," Raja lied.

"And that's the truth?"

"The absolute truth," Raja said and smiled.

Aryan knew Raja was lying. But he needed that lie right now. They both understood it. That lie was important, it was necessary. For sometimes even an obvious lie could make us feel better even when we were aware of the truth for we refuse to believe in that truth and choose instead to trust a blatant lie as that lie comforted us and provided us with a refuge and kept us safe and protected us. That lie was absolutely vital.

Aryan quickly turned toward Raja and embraced him tightly. Raja took a moment to recover and then he embraced Aryan back.

They continued walking back to their respective homes having decided to meet each other in the evening. Aryan felt hungry while walking home and so he stopped at a roadside tea stall and drank a small cup of strong tea and ate some homemade biscuits. Then he continued walking home.

Aryan knew now that the course of his life would change once again. He knew that in the days that were to come he would forget all about Mumbai and he would forget all about painting and he would get back to the job he was destined to do.

Once again he would become a fisherman.

Read *The Barefoot Artist* (Book 2 in the Aryan Series) to continue with Aryan's journey:

Amazon US: https://www.amazon.com/dp/B0BWWHS41S

Amazon India: https://www.amazon.in/dp/B0BWWHS41S

Amazon UK: https://www.amazon.co.uk/dp/B0BWWHS41S

PLEASE LEAVE A REVIEW

Dear Reader,

If you liked and enjoyed this novel, I would like to request you to please take out some time and post a review on Amazon by visiting https://mybook.to/afishermansdream

As an independent writer, your review can help me and my books gain some credibility among readers and also help in driving sales.

I would greatly appreciate this gesture and it would only motivate me to continue writing.

Thank you for your support!

Regards,
Arthinkal

OTHER SERIES

Life in Kornur Series:

1. Untouchable Lives: A Literary and Social Novella (Book 1):

Amazon US: https://www.amazon.com/dp/B0C3JJ8B7X

Amazon India: https://www.amazon.in/dp/B0C3JJ8B7X

Amazon UK: https://www.amazon.co.uk/dp/B0C3JJ8B7X

2. Rumor Mill: A Literary and Social Novella (Book 2):

Amazon US: https://www.amazon.com/dp/B0C43V5VSM

Amazon India: https://www.amazon.in/dp/B0C43V5VSM

Amazon UK: https://www.amazon.co.uk/dp/
B0C43V5VSM

3. Changing Times: A Literary and Social Novella (Book 3):

Amazon US: https://www.amazon.com/dp/
B0C4M3W3FF

Amazon India: https://www.amazon.in/dp/
B0C4M3W3FF

Amazon UK: https://www.amazon.co.uk/dp/
B0C4M3W3FF

4. The Boy and the King: A Parable (Children's Philosophical Novella) (Standalone):

Amazon US: https://www.amazon.com/dp/
B0CGRFBCWX

Amazon India: https://www.amazon.in/dp/
B0CGRFBCWX

Amazon UK: https://www.amazon.co.uk/dp/
B0CGRFBCWX

ABOUT THE AUTHOR

ARTHINKAL

Arthinkal is a pseudonym for Jordan John Anthony, born in Mumbai, India. *A Fisherman's Dream* is my debut novel. I also maintain a weekly newsletter on which I post essays and articles on literature, music, art, history, philosophy, politics, law, and social issues.

Join my mailing list to receive a free copy of the first book in the *Life in Kornur Series*, *Untouchable Lives: A Novella*, by visiting https://arthinkal.substack.com/p/free-ebook-untouchable-lives-a-novella

You can also join my mailing list by subscribing to my weekly newsletter for new book updates and to receive my essays and articles in your inbox: https://arthinkal.substack.com/ (You can unsubscribe at any time if you wish to do so).

Your support would mean a lot to me in my journey as an independent writer.

Connect with me on:
Instagram: https://www.instagram.com/arthinkal_/
Twitter: https://twitter.com/arthinkal
My Newsletter: https://arthinkal.substack.com/
My Website: https://arthinkal.com/

he still battles with the crippling feelings of doubt and uncertainty, he feels prepared to go all the way until he finally makes it as an artist.

But will Aryan make it this time? Or will he give in to the temptation of quitting on himself and his long-held dream?

The Barefoot Artist is the second book in a literary fiction series and is a coming-of-age story about hope and never giving up. If you liked the first book in this series, A Fisherman's Dream, or The Alchemist by Paulo Coelho, then you will love this book.

Buy The Barefoot Artist to experience the emotions and struggles Aryan has to go through to realize his dream!

The Barefoot Artist (The Aryan Series: Book 2)

Untouchable Lives: A Novella (Life In Kornur Series Book 1)

Untouchable Lives is a novella written as a series of vignettes that chronicle the daily lives of manual scavengers, sewer cleaners, cow skinners, cobblers, and fishermen, all untouchable inhabitants in the coastal village of Kornur, India.

Untouchability is a social evil that has been a part of Indian society for centuries. It is the practice of ostracizing a group of people deemed as untouchables due to their low caste in the rigid and dogmatic caste system.

These vignettes highlight the plight of the untouchables. They portray the daily discrimination faced by them, the humiliation they have to endure, the dreadful and inhumane jobs they still continue to do due to tradition, their innocent ambitions and desires, and the small things that make them happy. Simultaneously, they also show the gradual development of a backward and secluded coastal village slowly transforming into a city against the wishes of its inhabitants.

These stories are based on similar incidents that occur quite often even to this day and deal with the subjects of ostracization, class, caste, etc.

Untouchable Lives is the first novella in a literary and social fiction series. If you like the works of John Steinbeck or Toni Morrison, then you will love this book.

Buy Untouchable Lives to experience and understand the lives of the most disenfranchised population in the Indian subcontinent today!

Rumor Mill: A Novella (Life In Kornur Series Book 2)

Rumor Mill is a novella written as a series of vignettes that chronicle the daily lives of tea vendors, rickshaw drivers, coconut tree climbers, landless farmers, and manual scavengers, all untouchable inhabitants in the coastal village of Kornur, India.

Rumor Mill is the second novella in a literary and social fiction series. If you like the works of John

Steinbeck or Toni Morrison, then you will love this book.

Buy Rumor Mill to experience and understand the lives of the most disenfranchised population in the Indian subcontinent today!

Changing Times: A Novella (Life In Kornur Series Book 3)

Changing Times is a novella written as a series of vignettes that chronicle the daily lives of school children, the celebration of the harvest festival of the village, and the gradual development of a backward and secluded coastal village slowly transforming into a city against the wishes of its inhabitants.

Changing Times is the third novella in a literary and social fiction series. If you like the works of R.K. Narayan and Rabindranath Tagore, then you will love this book.

Buy Changing Times to experience the simple and interesting lives of the inhabitants of a small coastal village in India!

Made in the USA
Monee, IL
23 September 2024

66409524R00125